make them shrink to tolerable proportions,
the good one hopes to accomplish shrinks also."

Francis Marion Beynon's autobiographical novel *Aleta Dey*
is increasingly recognized as a small classic of early
twentieth-century fiction. Beynon was a journalist and
feminist much involved in public affairs in early
twentieth-century Manitoba. In 1917, aged 33, she
was forced to leave her job as a result of her open pacifism,
and she soon moved to New York where she dropped out
of the public eye. *Aleta Dey*, first published in 1919,
tells in plain and affecting prose the story of a girl
growing up in Manitoba, becoming politically conscious,
and falling in love with McNair, a man of much
more conventional views. World War I brings a crisis
for them both after McNair enlists as a soldier.

Though Beynon was a Canadian, her spare, emotionally
open prose may have less in common with that of other
Canadian writers of the time than it does with the style
of contemporaneous western American women writers
such as Willa Cather and Laura Ingalls Wilder.
Like Cather's *My Antonia*, Beynon's *Aleta Dey*
resonates with prairie simplicity, passion, and strength.

cover: 'Celebration on the Streets, September, 1918'.
Photographer unknown.

ALETA DEY

Francis Marion Beynon

broadview press

Canadian Cataloguing in Publication Data

Beynon, Francis Marion, 1884–1951
    Aleta Dey

"Encore editions from Broadview Press"
ISBN 1-55111-391-0

I. Title.

PS8503.E94A78 2000   C813'.52   C00-932229-9
PR9199.3.B4245A78 2000

Broadview Press Ltd., is an independent, international publishing house, incorporated in 1985.

North America:
P.O. Box 1243, Peterborough, Ontario, Canada K9J 7H5
3576 California Road, Orchard Park, NY 14127
Tel: (705) 743-8990; Fax: (705) 743-8353
E-mail: customerservice@broadviewpress.com

United Kingdom:
Turpin Distribution Services Ltd.,
Blackhorse Rd, Letchworth, Hertfordshire SG6 1HN
Tel: (1462) 672555; Fax: (1462) 480947
E-mail: turpin@rsc.org

Australia:
St. Clair Press, P.O. Box 287, Rozelle, NSW 2039
Tel: (02) 818-1942; Fax: (02) 418-1923

www.broadviewpress.com

Broadview Press gratefully acknowledges the financial support of the Book Publishing Industry Development Program, Ministry of Canadian Heritage, Government of Canada.

PRINTED IN THE UNITED STATES

PREFACE

Though the winds of popular caprice are almost as variable as those of nature it did not seem possible back in the dark days of military tyranny, when this book was written, that the day would come in the lifetime of any radical then living, when the tables would be turned over a large portion of a great continent.

But so it is today, and with the radicals in the saddle in several European countries, we see the sorry spectacle of history repeating itself and the oppressed becoming the oppressor. My mind refuses to make any distinction between the tyranny of radicals and the tyranny of conservatives. As I see it, tyranny wears many wigs, but he has only one complexion.

It is neither excuse nor palliation of this tendency to suppress conservative opinion to say that they are only getting their own back. Revenge is the meager dream of little minds. It is like the remembered table delights of our childhood, which when repeated in maturity are flat and unpalatable.

Perhaps if the conservative mind would show that it had learned anything from this great upheaval the situation would be some-what relieved. But regrettably it does not. It has not even sufficient honesty to face the fact that the anarchy it hates is the logical conclusion of the war which it loved.

The militarist felt that he had the pacifist in a difficult position when he asked him if he would stand by and see his mother murdered. And he had. It would have been conclusive were it not that the militarist was not one whit less willing to face the logical conclusion of war—which is that it is our duty to murder anyone whose conduct and opinions seem to us to be injurious to the state in which we live—that, indeed, we need only notify the Almighty that he is on our side to make it a religious obligation.

The New York alderman who said he would not hesitate to murder traitors to the flag was at least partially consistent; to be fully so he would have to admit that it was the duty of any other citizen, who felt his opinions were injurious, to murder him. Likely as not he would boggle at that.

And that is anarchy, if you please.

But as I did not believe in war, and the anarchistic methods of war governments, neither do I believe in revolution and the oppressive measures of revolutionary governments. It is not possible for any group of people in a country either to inspire or to feel the emotion of fear without spiritually degrading the whole. So it is imperative that the most rampant militarist, imperialist and royalist be protected in the right of everyman to think his honest thoughts aloud, even if to insure this some of us, whom in their day of power they so ruthlessly suppressed have once again to take up the heavy burden of rowing against the tide of public opinion, sweeping along as furiously as before in the narrow channels of bigotry.

But only so can we ourselves be free, for whether we

like it or not, our spirits are chained to the most craven in the country and the limitation of their dreams contracts our own horizon.

THE AUTHOR

CONTENTS

CHAPTER I.
A Coward.

I am a coward.

I think I was born to be free, but my parents, with God as one of their chief instruments of terror, frightened me into servility. Perhaps I owe it to the far horizons of my Canadian prairie birth-place; perhaps to the furious tempests that rocked our slim wooden dwelling, or it may be to the untrammelled migration of birds to distant lands that the shame of being a coward has survived their chastening. I know that these things have always beckoned to something in me that vainly beat its wings against the bars of life.

Mother and father began when Jean and I were barely out of the cradles to perform a task called "breaking our spirit," which seemed to them essential to our well-being. My mother did it reluctantly, from a stern sense of Christian duty, but my father seemed to take a solid satisfaction in the work. Between them they succeeded so well that now when my employer rings for me my first sensation is always fear.

It is wonderful how early one can be made into a coward. I was one at five. I remember a golden summer morning when the milk pans were all about the kitchen and flies were buzzing between them and the window. Jean was tugging at my hair and I slapped her hands and said,

"Darn you, stop that."

Mother's portly figure revolved until she was facing me.

"What did you say, Aleta?" she demanded sharply.

"Nothing," I answered, looking down at my copper-toed shoes.

"She said 'Darn you,'" Jean put in, with a self-righteous smirk.

Mother picked me up; set me in my high chair and promised to whip me at noon.

It was a long, long morning, and I spent most of it in bitter plans for revenge. If mother were one of those flies I'd stamp on her and squash her into nothing. I'd run away and drown myself in the big pond and then she'd be sorry, and I'd be glad if she was. So I thought and thought as I boiled internally with childish rage and impotence.

After a long time she took a strap down from a nail behind the door. All at once I ceased to be angry and became afraid. I did not want to be struck. Mother came over and set me down on the floor. I thought she looked very ugly as she stood over me with the strap in her hands.

"Hold out your right hand," she commanded. I hesitated. I did not want to, but I could see that she meant to strike me somewhere, so I held it out. She brought the strap down on it smartly twice, and I whimpered.

"Now the left."

She slapped that twice.

"Are you sorry you said darn?" she inquired in a threatening voice.

I thought a moment and found I was not, so I said nothing.

"You must not get stubborn," she insisted, and began

slapping me harder and faster, and the harder she slapped, the less sorry I felt.

But she was determined to have the lie, so at last, when my hands were all red and stinging and I was choking with sobs, I whispered between catches in my breath, "I'm sorry," and she stopped. God knows I wouldn't have done it only I was so very little and it was the only way to stop her.

But I was still ashamed to meet the big wind when I went out to play, and I tried to show him I was not a coward by shaking my little fist at the house and shouting, "I'm not sorry, and I hate you—I hate you—I hate you."

I was not at all sure that I deceived the wind. I suspected that he knew all the time that I was a coward.

Having learned physical fear so young it is no wonder that I lacked the courage to commit suicide on the morning of my christening, which happened that autumn. Through a peculiar set of circumstances, long since forgotten, I had missed being christened in infancy, so it was arranged that the Rev. Foster Forsyth, the Methodist minister, should come out on a certain day and rectify the omission.

"He'll set you in the middle of the room and turn a bucket of water over you," declared Letty, our hired girl.

I was aghast and ran to mother to ask about it. She was not a cruel woman, and usually she did not allow us to be frightened, but I think she did not understand my alarm and mortification in this case. She just laughed and said nothing, either way.

I met our hired man John coming in from the barn and asked him about it, and he, too, laughed and said a bath would do me good.

John was a remittance man. In the beginning England sent her younger sons of great families to Canada, and her criminals to Australia, and judging by some of the results our cousin had an unfair advantage over us.

How we born Canadians detested those English remittance men! Mr. A. G. Gardiner mentions in one of his books the days when it was not disrespectful to speak of "the colonies," and by the tone of his remarks one feels that he cannot understand the resentment felt by the overseas dominions at the use of the expression.

If Mr. Gardiner could have heard John say to my father, as I did, "You colonials, what do you know?" he would begin to comprehend.

My father combed the chaff out of his beard and answered, "Well, my man, I know how to plough a straight furrow."

"And that is about all you do know," John retorted contemptuously.

It was not quite fair. My father was not an educated man in the Englishman's sense of the word, but he took a deep interest in politics and kept himself well informed on the questions of the day. Moreover, we Canadians had a theory that it was a breach of the law of courtesy to tell people so bluntly of their shortcomings, and of the law of democracy to set oneself up as a judge of one's fellow men. When help became more plentiful our advertisements, like those of most of our neighbours, used to read, "No Englishman need apply."

I am sorry for those English remittance men now, at a distance of years from contact with them. Our crude way of living must have been as distasteful to them as their avowed contempt for everything we did, thought and had was to us.

But I was too young then to philosophise, and John's heartless laugh at my childish anxiety over my christening, was very unjustly, chalked up in my child mind against England.

I cannot explain the horror I felt at the thought of the public humiliation that had to be faced on the day of my christening. As the time approached my terror grew. On the night before it was to happen I found sleep impossible. I felt I could not lie awake in the dark and think of it, so I poked Jean in the side.

"Jean, Jean," I whispered.

Jean shut her mouth, turned her fair head the other way about on the pillow; opened her mouth and began to snore.

"Jean," I insisted, shaking her resolutely.

She opened her blue eyes and looked at me dreamily, "Is it morning?" she asked.

"Shssh!" I whispered. "It isn't morning."

"Then what for did you waken me?"

I slipped my arm about her neck. "Jean, do you think they'll pour a bucket of water over me to-morrow?"

"Letty said they would," she confirmed my terror.

I began to cry and Jean sat up in bed and put her arms around me in a motherly fashion, for she was a year my senior.

"Don't cry, Aleta," she begged, "don't cry. Maybe it won't hurt much."

There was poor comfort in that and I wept more and more bitterly.

Presently Jean slipped out of bed and fumbled about the bureau. When she came back she pressed her string of amber beads into my hand.

"You can have my beads if you won't cry," she promised. I slipped them under my pillow and we fell asleep locked in each other's arms.

But I wakened with the consciousness of impending disaster, which in its fullest detail rushed back into my mind. I was going to be christened to-day.

As I have said I cannot explain the horror I felt at the prospect of being set in the midst of a roomful of adults and having a bucket of water poured over me. I was sure I could never be happy again if it happened.

After breakfast I stole away by myself to the big pond. The heavy dew on the grass made my feet sopping wet, as I went out alone to die. I had fully made up my mind to jump into the pond, but when I came to the edge and looked down I was afraid. The water looked cold and dirty. I did not want to die, especially when mother was making lemon pies for dinner. But I could not bear the thought of what was to happen after dinner.

I stopped beside a scrubby little bush we children called the snowberry, the fruit of which was reputed to be poisonous. We had been warned repeatedly that if we ate those berries we should die. Here was an easier way out than by jumping into the dirty slimy pond. I gathered a handful of the berries. They were little silvery grey white things, which looked harmless enough, and I shoved the whole handful into my mouth.

Then I became afraid. I spat them out upon the ground and ran as fast as I could to the house for a cup of water, which I took out behind the gooseberry bushes and used to rinse my mouth. All the rest of the day I spent listening for trouble internally, so that the dread of the approaching christening became secondary.

When it was over I said to Jean, "Huh, you thought the preacher was going to pour a bucket of water over my head."

This was too much for Jean's patience. "You thought so, too," she insisted, "and you were awfully scared." "I wasn't scared," I contradicted her flatly.

We were playing in the sand-pile with Minnie Forsyth and Amy Cotter, whose mothers had brought them along to my christening. Minnie created a diversion at this juncture by announcing, "I heard my ma tell my pa your mother is going to have a baby."

Jean and I gasped.

"I know, the stork brings them," Amy explained.

Minnie sat back on her heels after having rounded off a mud pie, and said contemptuously, "Silly, that's not the way babies come." And there, while we knelt open mouthed around her in the sand-pile, she explained to us, with illustrations drawn from the farmyard, the main facts of procreation.

That night when mother was putting me to bed I asked abruptly, "Mother, where do babies come from?"

"The stork brings them," she answered, giving me a quick suspicious look.

"And where does the stork get them?" I persisted, in order to see if she would keep on lying.

Mother blushed. "In heaven," she snapped. "Don't ask so many questions."

I looked at mother's figure thoughtfully. I did not so much mind being a liar, now that I knew mother was one too. I wondered if God would let her go to heaven when she died. I hoped so, for I loved mother.

CHAPTER II.
Baby Brother.

It was winter. The snow was piled higher than my head, in places higher than my father's also, along the garden fence, and the windows were thick with frost. Mother used to take a flat iron from the stove and thaw them off, because it made the room dark. We slept with such heavy coverings on our bed that we wakened tired with the weight of them, and gathering up our clothes ran down to the kitchen stove to dress.

One day of that winter stands out alone in my memory. It was so cold that the kitchen door creaked ominously on its hinges when father went in or out to his chores. He was alone now, for John had gone to the town to work during the winter.

Mother went often to the window and looked out. She moved slowly, as if she were very tired. Once I tagged along and climbed up on a chair and looked out too. There was nothing to see but the snow drifting in big, loose white waves for miles upon miles, to where the level white fields met the blue rim of the sky.

Mother put her arm about me; drew me close to her side, and ran her cracked fingers through my curly red brown hair.

"If mother should have to go away and leave Aleta she would be a good girl, wouldn't she?" she asked.

I put my arms about her neck and clung there desperately "I'll tell God not to let you go away," I remonstrated.

"Do you think it will be to-day?" Letty asked, from the table, where she was making cookies.

"I don't know," mother answered, and sighed a long weary shuddering sigh. "I hope not. It would be a terrible day for Jack to go for the doctor."

When she spoke again her voice was sharp and irritable. "Letty, do take that pot of feed of the stove. The smell of it makes me sick."

Jean and I were sewing for our dolls over in a corner, but when mother went to the window again, an hour or two later, I put down the doll's frock and followed her.

All was changed outside. The sky had grown dark and the snow drifted past in solid white sheets, so that one could not see even the garden fence.

"You can't go away," I said jubilantly, "look how it storms."

Mother raised my little brown hand to her lips and kissed it. "One would think she knew something was the matter," she murmured.

When I came back Jean said, "Why don't you sit still and sew?"

"I hate sewing," I answered.

"You're lazy," she said.

Perhaps she was right.

*　　*　　*　　*　　*

It was the middle of the night when I was awakened by a loud cry. I sat up in bed shaking. The cry came again

—a fearful agonized sound. I do not know how I knew it was my mother crying. The screams died away into a sob that was even more unbearable to listen to.

I slipped out of bed and trotted into the hall in my bare feet. Letty was just coming out of my mother's room.

"Go back to bed right away, Aleta," she commanded me sharply.

"I want my mother," I whimpered.

"God help you, child; I'm afraid your mother is dying and your father is lost in the storm."

"Where's father?" I asked.

"Gone for the doctor. Run back to bed quickly."

I pretended to start for my room, but when she had gone on downstairs with the kettle I tip-toed back and shoved mother's door open a crack. I looked just once. I did not want to look any more. I ran back to bed, where I shivered and sobbed so hard I wakened Jean.

She started up in a fright. "What's the matter?" she asked anxiously.

"Mother's dying and father's lost. Letty says so."

I tried three times to tell her of what I had seen in mother's room, but could not. This is the first time in all these years that I have been able to speak of it.

Jean began to cry too, and I sobbed out, "Mother, mother, mother!" over and over again. Sometime we both held our breath there in the dark and listened to the wind howling around the house and rattling the window panes.

I don't know which of us fell asleep first, but our next consciousness was that it was morning and the sun was streaming in through our window. Nobody had come to waken us.

Then we remembered about father and mother and got out of bed crying to ourselves; gathered our clothes and started for the stairs.

As we passed mother's door her voice called out to us, "Girls, come here."

Jean rushed in, but I was afraid to go.

"Come, Aleta," mother called again, and I went shyly in. She was lying in a nice clean bed, and on the pillow beside her there was a wee head.

"Kiss your baby brother," mother suggested.

I did and it made me feel very queer. "Let me hold him," I begged.

"You're too small yet," mother said. "You'll have more than you want of holding him," she added, with her dry cynicism.

She was wrong in that. I think if Barry could be questioned he would agree that her prophecy was never fulfilled.

A big strange man came into the room then, and we remembered about father. Mother told us he had reached home safely and sent us out of the room.

We went downstairs, and shortly afterwards father came in from the stable. He was a tall, stocky man with bushy whiskers. This morning he wore an air of great importance. He went round about to kick several chairs and Rover out of his way.

CHAPTER III.
God in the Storm.

The following summer they sent me to Sunday School, but that did not improve my opinion of God. The being I heard about there was always angry at somebody about something, and I was afraid of him. There are good people who claim to have met the God of the big quiet places and the starry heavens in churches, but personally I never have. The God I met there wore an expression which I have since seen on the faces of stage policemen applying the third degree to a criminal.

But I met him one afternoon the summer I was nine, in a corner of the pasture field. Mother and father had gone to town, and while Jean sewed a rip in Barry's shirt I went out in the strange brooding hush before a thunderstorm to find the cows.

From the blue black sky, resting evenly, like a bowl, upon the level floor of earth, filtered a weird shadowy twilight, and I looked east and west and south, and there was nothing but a few shacks between me and the far away edge of the world. I felt very tiny under that immense black dome, and I was glad even of the barbed wire fence which shut me in from those immeasurable distances.

The bluebells hung tense on their slender stems, and the last whisper had died away among the stunted poplar scrub. Over in the east a yellow snake of fire wiggled down the sky, followed by a crash that seemed to rock the world. A breeze came by. It stirred my hair, ran along the grass at my feet and set all the lilies and bluebells to nodding. Then all was still again and dark, but I felt as if I were riding on the wings of a bird. I know God passed by in that breeze, because for a little while I was not afraid of father or mother, or of anything in the whole world.

But perhaps that is not quite true, for I do not believe I would have had the courage to write in a composition at school any of the strange new things I thought as I drove the cattle home in that queer dark hush before the storm.

The next thing the world must evolve is protective coloration for souls, so that society and our public schools will not be able to pounce upon and trample into the mire of conventionality all the hopeful little buds of inspiration which spring up in children's minds.

CHAPTER IV.
Lightning.

As I neared the house Jean came running to meet me. Her face was as white as chalk, and tears streamed down her cheeks.

"The house has been struck by lightening," she wailed, "and—and I think—its killed Barry."

Everything that happened after that is like a dream. I vaguely remember running like the wind, with Jean panting beside me. I hardly glanced at the torn and blackened wall, but ran straight to the couch where Jean had dragged his limp little body. He was absolutely still. The little hand, with the dimpled knuckles hung over the side of the couch; the fair head was twisted awkwardly to one side.

I caught him in my arms and almost shook him as I cried, "Barry, Barry, waken up quick. Leta wants you."

The small limp figure lay quiet against my shoulder. He did not put the fat little arms about my neck and whisper, as usual, "Barry loves Leta."

Child though I was I can remember yet the sick thought that he would never do that again; that I would never waken up to find him sitting on my chest or poking his little fingers into my eyes and saying, "I sought you'd never waken up."

"Do you think he's dead?" Jean whispered.

I could not speak, so I just nodded over Barry's little fair head.

"I saw Mary White when she fainted at the Sunday School picnic," Jean said, "and they threw cold water on her face, and she got all right."

I put Barry down, and we both ran for the water pail. It was empty, but we took hold of the handle together and ran to the well. It was very dark now, and long wicked chains of lightning ran about the sky at intervals of seconds, while a white light played without intermission along the horizon, and the thunder grumbled continuously, breaking out occasionally into loud crashes. The chip-strewn yard, littered with farm machinery and hen coops, was lighted by a fitful glare. I noticed that all the fowls and animals had crowded into shelter.

Sobbing with terror of the thing that had happened to Barry and of the storm, we pumped and pumped until we had filled the pail, and then dragged it between us to the house, splashing the water over our slippers and little print skirts.

With shaking hands Jean filled the dipper and carried it to the couch. Barry was lying just as we had left him.

"Would you throw it all over him?" she whispered anxiously.

"I don't know," I said; "what did they do to Mary?"

"I just forget," she answered, "but I think they threw a lot." Whereupon she turned the whole contents of the dipper over Barry's face.

He lay as still as before.

I snatched up the dipper and brought it full again and dashed it over him.

The limp little figure continued motionless so I ran frantically for a third. Before I reached the bench, Jean gave a cry, the inflection of which stays with me to this moment. When I reached the couch Barry's head was stirring on the pillow. Jean and I rubbed his hands and called to him, and presently he opened his dark blue eyes and began to cry.

We took him up out of the water, and Jean ran to get dry clothes to put on him. We were too much excited to think of the storm which was roaring and threshing about our prairie dwelling.

By the time we had Barry undressed and into clean clothes the storm had passed. When he stood up on my lap and buried his damp fair head in the hollow of my neck I looked through the open door at the clean, newly-washed world, twinkling and laughing in the sunlight. I laughed, too, but that night I had dreams of losing Barry, and wakened over and over to clutch his warm little body.

CHAPTER V.
School in Town.

We moved, I think it was the following spring, to a farm on the outskirts of a little village called Souris River. Jean and I were allowed to go on ahead with the first load of furniture on a pledge of good behaviour until mother arrived. We pranced up and down and promised anything she asked.

The roads were so bad that the wagon crept along, but the ploughed fields, freshly cleared of snow, were fragrant under the mid-March sun, and we were adventuring forth into a new life.

Always I have loved the up grade of the year, the thrill of a new awakening, even though it is at this season more than any other that I am conscious of that something within which struggles hopelessly to break the bonds of life and find its way to freedom.

The new home seemed to me quite wonderful. The house was big, very big, I thought, for it had a front hall, and there was an archway between the parlour and the dining room, and there was a big sunny L of a kitchen. I was particularly elated over the archway, for it was just like Minnie Forsyth's and other places in town, and already I had begun to accept the world's dictum that the usual is necessarily the beautiful.

Jean and I were sitting out on the front steps a week

or two later when two little girls passed, staring very hard at us. We stared back at them. When the reached the end of the fence they turned about and marched up to the gate.

"How much is your gape seed a pound?" they inquired simultaneously. Then they took to their heels and ran as fast as they could towards town. We put down our dolls and ran after them.

When they reached the culvert over the ravine they halted, and stood digging the toes of their shoes into the loose black soil of the country road.

"What did you say that for?" Jean asked, when we had come within speaking distance.

The older girl laughed amiably. "Just for fun," she answered. "What's your name?"

We exchanged names and ages and found that the strangers were May and Pauline Ransome, and that the former was a year older than Jean and Pauline a year older than myself. Their father was a doctor, and they were Presbyterians. This last was a great blow, as it eliminated all hope of meeting them at Sunday School. It also, though this worried us little, put aside any chance of encountering them in heaven, for already I understood vaguely that Presbyterians, leaning on the false prop of fore-ordination, were heading straight for the burning fiery furnace.

"What grade are you in at school?" May asked.

Jean and I looked at each other uncomfortably. "We've only been to school two winters," Jean answered shyly.

The strangers made no attempt to conceal their amazement.

"You'll have to go in the baby class," May said, "and

everybody will laugh at you. I wouldn't be in your place for anything."

I could feel my lip tremble as I thought of the unpleasantness ahead. Then Pauline leaned over and planted a kiss upon my forehead.

"May and I won't laugh," she promised, "and you'll soon get ahead."

Jean's face lighted up at that. "Oh, yes," she said easily, "we're very bright and we'll soon catch up."

For my part I just squeezed Pauline's hand very hard and said nothing, but I was greatly comforted. I had found a friend.

And I needed one. I have never forgotten the unpleasantness of those first few months at school. It was not being behind girls of my own age that made me unhappy, for my more mature mind made promotion come easily, but being hedged about by a wall of unrelated don'ts.

One morning after the teacher had read a chapter from the Bible I put up my hand and was permitted to speak. "How did God learn to use such beautiful words?" I asked, accepting the Bible literally as the word of God. I can see that room to this day. The sunlight filtering through the scrawny geraniums of the window sill lit up the rows of still little figures. I can hear yet the hush that followed my question.

Then the teacher laughed and the children tittered. Already the public school had taught us to titter when authority laughs, which is one of its great functions in society.

"That is a very foolish question, Aleta," the teacher said, dismissing it, and my fellow students looked at me pityingly. I glanced across at Pauline. She was not laughing, but she looked shocked and troubled.

"Attention!" the teacher exclaimed, sharply.

We turned our heads straight to the front and put our feet evenly on the floor.

"Books out; one, two, three."

In three exactly uniform movements we placed our hands on each side of our exercise books, drew them towards us and slid them on to the desk. The day had begun.

All morning I worked away with an under-current of resentment that my wonder at the compelling beauty of the Biblical language should have been turned into an occasion for derision.

I cannot remember the time when the melodious measures of the old Hebrew poets did not delight my ear, although I understood only a sentence or two here and there.

When father was away from home mother used to read for prayers, always selecting some of those especially lilting passages from the Psalms, Isaiah or Ecclesiastes, particularly from the latter that magnificent picturesque chapter beginning "Remember now thy Creator in the days of thy youth …"

Father's favourite passages were: "Honour thy father and thy mother," and "Wives submit yourselves unto your own husbands." He never failed to read this advice of Paul's when he and mother had had a quarrel.

CHAPTER VI.
Punishment.

There was a big boy in Pauline's class called Ned Grant, whom I liked. He never laughed at me for what the rest called my queer questions, which popped out sometimes in spite of myself, though at longer and longer intervals.

Ned Grant's father was an American Socialist and agnostic, who, after losing his wife, had come west and taken a farm adjoining the one to which we moved.

Theoretically mother did not approve of him, but she enjoyed his conversation more than that of most of her neighbours, and she mended for him and his son, and made their bread. Her practical tolerance so far outran her theories of conduct that in spite of her narrow code of morality she counted her friends among all classes and sects.

So partly on account of mother's kindness; partly because of his own radical upbringing, I could always count on Ned's support. I needed it less and less, however, as I learned through a long process of humiliation that one may ask questions at school about arithmetic, spelling, geography, and the dates of history, but one must not inquire and it is immoral to think about the genesis of life, God, except in certain set phrases, or the spirit of history.

Minnie Forsyth, who is now a missionary to the poor long suffering Chinese, had a knack of always asking the right kind of question. I recollect that she looked up in the teacher's face one day and asked sweetly, "Please, teacher, does God love me?"

The teacher answered sanctimoniously, "Yes, dear, God loves everyone: only of course there are some who are naughty and have to be punished," she added quickly, as if God's unmeasured love might be too great a license to happiness.

Minnie responded properly, "Thank you, teacher dear."

The Psalmist exclaimed in apparent surprise, "Why do the heathen rage?" I know one reason.

I, on the contrary, always asked the forbidden thing. Our teacher read a chapter one morning in which one of the prophets, in the name of the Lord, threatened a tribe with complete annihilation at the outset, and at the end assured them that the Lord had turned away his wrath from them.

When she had finished I inquired in all sincerity, "Teacher" (I could never be brought to use that servile form of address, "Please, teacher"), "does God often change His mind?"

She looked "the lake that burneth forever" at me. Immediately the class, taking its cue from her, fixed its eyes upon me with a "poor lost soul" expression.

"Aleta, you are a very irreverent little girl," she said, in a voice of awful solemnity. "God doesn't love little girls who are irreverent."

Then she adjusted her spectacles over her pale blue eyes and went on with her work. I felt a poke at my elbow, and the girl behind me handed me a note. It was from Ned Grant. He said, "You're a brick, Aleta."

That evening Pauline, May and Ned walked home with Jean and me. It was a perfect June day. The sky was so brilliant one could not bear to look up at it, and the flower-dotted grass along the road allowance made a lovely fresco for the dark billowy fields of grain.

Much to my discomfort Ned deliberately brought up the question I had asked in the morning.

"Miss Black thinks she knows all about God and the Bible, doesn't she?" he asked.

"Well, I think Aleta's question was sort of disrespectful," Pauline said. "I don't think you should ask questions like that about God." She swung along the dusty road decisively, a somber, black-haired, dark-eyed, long-limbed girl.

"Why not?" Ned inquired. His voice was contemptuous, for there had long been a mutual dislike between him and Pauline.

"Because it's wrong."

Pauline flushed angrily, and was about to speak when May, who was in the room above ours, interrupted, "What are you talking about?" she questioned.

When she was told she disposed of the matter in a sentence. "The teacher ought to have spanked you, Aleta."

"No, she oughtn't," said Jean. Then she changed the subject.

Barry came running out to meet us. "Mother's making lemon tarts," he called, "and she said you could bring Pauline and Ned and May in to have some."

He named our guests in the order of his own preference. Already he was standing in the circle of Pauline's arms, giving her a "love."

"You're Pauline's boy, aren't you?" she asked.

"I'm Leta's boy first, then Jean's and then Pauline's," he answered.

We walked on, Pauline and I, each holding a moist, dirty little hand, except when Barry withdrew it to tuck the bottom of his blue duck blouse inside his little pants.

After the tarts we went out to play about the barn. This was always a treat to the village children, and we, who were poor and had so few things to show off with, were rather proud to have this advantage over them.

We were climbing up and sliding down a haystack when father came along. He had been very sullen since morning, when a man had come to see him about a mortgage. Now he flew into a terrible rage.

"What are you children doing there?" he roared.

We scrambled out of the haystack and stood before him, our hair and dresses full of straw.

"Who told you to bring these youngsters here?" he demanded, his eyes turning from Jean to me.

"Mother said we might," Jean answered, meekly.

"Your mother ought to know better then," he retorted fiercely, "Go on home with you," he continued, turning to our guests, "I'm not going to have a lot of kids tearing my haystack to pieces."

They went. And we stood trembling with rage and fear before him. I cannot express the bitter humiliation of having our guests dismissed in this way.

"I'll teach you," he raged; "I'll teach you to bring a lot of youngsters around here to destroy things."

He went around the corner of the barn and came back in a moment with a stick.

"Hold out your hand," he said to Jean. She did, and he made six dark welts on it with the stick. Jean screamed.

"Now the other one."

His fury and brutality were rising, and he brought the blood on this hand. Jean's screams were terrible, and Barry ran wailing to the house.

I was sick with fear at the sight of this human creature, mad with the lust for physical conquest over anything that stood in his way. Had I been brave I would have defied him, but I was very little and terribly afraid. So I ran as fast as I could and crawled into a hole in the haystack. I did not know then that one should never run from an infuriated animal unless one is sure one can run faster.

Father ran after me and dragged me out by the foot. He was pale, and his face was working horribly. He did not wait to ask that I hold out my hand, but struck me furiously and indiscriminately with the stick.

"Are you sorry you've been a bad girl?" he kept demanding hoarsely, between blows.

Sorry! The one thought in my mind at that moment was murder. There is no more horrible spectacle than that of a human being drunk with the desire for victory over the body of another human being. The revolting thing is that in reverting himself to the emotions of the jungle he drags his victim down with him to the level of a beast of prey. We, the attacker and the attacked, were for the time being on the spiritual plane of the tiger and the ape.

"Are you sorry?" he roared.

Still I said nothing. I was too much of a coward to defy him, but he had overdone the brutality, and even my craven heart was roused to a passive resistance.

I screamed at the top of my voice, and presently mother came from the house and said "Jack, you must stop whipping that child."

"You go away and mind your business," father snapped, but in a wavering voice.

Mother came up and looked him straight in the eye. Then she took the stick from him and threw it as far as she could throw. I remember how her tight black alpaca waist slipped up away from her skirt, as she raised her plump brown arm, on which the sleeve was rolled up to the elbow. She was a little roly poly woman with plain features, of which mine are a duplicate, but at that moment she was magnificent. A soul had come into the jungle.

Jean and I had been wrought up to such a pitch of nervous excitement that we sobbed short, dry sobs all the evening, and lay staring into the dark long after we had finished our lessons and gone to bed.

Suddenly there flashed into my mind a picture of father getting down on his knees after supper, as he always did, and praying. I saw him very vividly, with a hand on each side of a well-scrubbed kitchen chair, and his beard tilted towards the ceiling, as he thanked God for keeping him from sin during the day.

"Did you hear him praying to God?" I whispered to Jean.

"And after he'd been such a pig," Jean agreed.

"If he goes to heaven I don't want to; I'd rather go to hell," I exclaimed, growing more reckless, and yet secretly hoping that the devil wasn't listening, and would not take too prompt an advantage of my preference.

Barry sat up in his cot and looked about him. Then there was a patter of little bare feet on the floor, as he climbed up and cuddled his warm little body against mine.

"Never mind, Leta," he whispered; "when I'm a man I'll get a gun and shoot him dead, so I will."

"No, Barry dear, you can't do that," I whispered back regretfully, "because they would put you in jail or hang you."

"What are you children talking about?" father's voice asked sharply from the door, where he had come to spy upon us. It was a peculiarity of his that he wanted the sensual satisfaction of a physical victory together with the respect which belongs to a spiritual one.

CHAPTER VII.
The Spiritual X-Ray.

From around the corner of the barn one evening in my twelfth summer Jean and I saw Mr. Elton, the Methodist minister, drive into the yard. We watched mother come out to speak to him, rolling down her sleeves as she came; watched him get down from the seat and begin to unhitch his long-haired bay horse from the shabbily respectable buggy, which so well matched up with his dingy black ministerial coat. Then we effaced ourselves from the landscape.

"Let's go and play in the willows beside the pond," Jean suggested.

I looked up into her round rosy-cheeked face, with its halo of golden hair, and we laughed.

As fast as we could we ran for the willows. "Do you suppose we could hear her now if she called?' I asked.

Jean's answer was not as irrelevant as it sounded. "She'll likely get me to set the table, and make some muffins, and send you in to talk to him," she reflected aloud with satisfaction.

I stood up, holding a bunch of white anemones I had just gathered in my hand and rubbed the yellow pollen against my nose, as I asked shyly, "Jean, what do you say when he looks at you so hard and asks if you are right with God?"

"I say 'yes' every time," Jean answered, "and then he stops worrying me, but I don't like him to do it."

"Neither do I," I agreed. "How does anyone know whether they are right with God?"

"I don't know."

"Do you suppose anybody, even Mr. Elton, really knows?" I questioned.

Mother's voice calling, "Girls, girls," interrupted us.

Reluctantly we turned our feet houseward. When we entered the big grey-painted kitchen, with the flourishing red geraniums in the window, mother, who was bustling about getting tea, stopped and said, "Aleta, go into the parlour and talk to Mr. Elton."

"I showed him all the photos last time," I objected.

"Then just talk to him, dear," she answered, and her blue eyes twinkled as she bent and kissed my forehead.

When mother asked me that way to do anything I was helpless to resist. I would have faced a regiment of Eltons.

While Mr. Elton pumped my hand up and down he gave me a deep, silent, searching look, which made me squirm inwardly.

"How is Minnie?" I asked desperately, resolved to ward of the spiritual inquisition as long as possible. Minnie Forsyth was boarding with the Eltons in order to continue at a good school, her father having been moved by the Methodist Board to a less desireable town. I seized upon her eagerly as a plausible subject of conversation. "Minnie is very well, but the question is, how is Aleta?" he said pointedly.

I understood his meaning perfectly, but pretended not to. "I'm fine," I answered, "but I had an awfully sore throat on Monday and one of my tonsils is swelled up yet."

He stared at me in funereal silence.

"Would you like to look at it," I offered amiably.

He waived aside the invitation to explore my throat. "It wasn't your body I was asking about, child; it was your immortal soul."

He had taken a seat on the horsehair sofa, and I sat forward on the prickly edge of a horsehair chair, one small hand on each knee, and looked at him solemnly.

He did not see, as I did, a big housefly, which, sighting his tempting bald crown from a distance, had come swooping across the room singing the Hallelujah Chorus. It circled round and round, like a hawk over a chicken, and just as he asked about my immortal soul it settled. He jumped up and rubbed it off.

"I'll run and get a piece of paper to kill it," I offered eagerly.

"Never mind, child," he called after me, but I was gone.

When I returned I chased that fly, or another, mercilessly. At first Mr. Elton looked on coldly and disapprovingly. Then he began to watch the fly and point it out to me. Finally he sprang up and snatched the swatter from my hand. Just as he flattened it against the window pane with a sharp slap mother appeared in the doorway and announced supper. My immortal soul had, for the time being, escaped the microscope.

Supper over, Mr. Elton asked for a Bible and after reading a Psalm, he knelt down and prayed. He prayed for us all, but for me in particular, advising God that he might need to keep an especial watch over me, as I had a tendency to an undisciplined spirit. There was a desperate earnestness in his voice, and when he went on to ask the Heavenly Father to surround us all with His loving protection he brought the tears to my eyes. I peeked through my fingers at him, and his face was shining with a strange light. He had opened a pathway to his God—a narrow-minded, bigoted, dogmatic God, it is true, for his very limited intelligence was not capable of drawing a great and splendid picture of God—but his God.

The next Wednesday evening at prayer meeting he took up the lesson of the foolish virgins and pointed out that they obviously were symbolized by the Presbyterians, Baptists and Church of England members. He did not bother to mention the Roman Catholics, for nobody in Souris River seriously expected them to go to heaven.

We had only one Roman Catholic family in the district, and it did seem to me hard that Mrs. Fagan should go straight down to hell when she got through raising her family, nursing her neighbours, and being jolly and kind to all us youngsters. But so they said it was written. She did the right things, but the poor woman did not believe the right things. Hence her lost condition.

On the way home from meeting I said to father, as we walked along the deep-rutted road in the moonlight. "Did you ever hear of such a thing as Mr. Elton calling the other churches foolish virgins?"

Father stroked his beard with placid satisfaction as he declared, "You've got to be converted and born again before you go to heaven, and they don't believe in it."

I looked over the shadowy rustling fields of grain and then up to the eternal stars, and said something which I intended to be very personal, while appearing casual.

"Some of them are very kind to their families and pleasant in their homes," I hinted.

Father gave a grunt of annoyance. "You don't know what you're talking about," he said shortly.

But I did, in a way. There must have been a time, for I was no intellectual prodigy, when I did not resent the assumption of infallibility on the part of any individual or group of individuals, but I cannot remember it. Among my earliest emotional recollections is the resentment I felt at the self-complacency of the holiness of the Methodists, who visited our home, and at my father's extreme partisanship in politics.

CHAPTER VIII.
Ned is Expelled.

It was the second summer of the Boer War, and the public feeling was inflamed with that peculiar national hysteria war breeds. I was in my fifteenth year, and Ned, eighteen and full grown, was studying for his second-class certificate. On a certain spring day, at the last recess, Ned, Pauline, Jean and I were sitting together in a group talking, when Pauline put her hand down on Ned's desk and picked up a copy of an American history, which Ned's father had brought with him from the land of his birth.

She tossed it disdainfully aside. "That book is full of lies," she declared contemptuously.

Ned flushed, but he merely reached over and took up his English history. "So is this," he said quietly.

I was dumbfounded. I had questioned my parents and the Bible, but up to that moment it had never occurred to me to doubt the English history.

Pauline grew purple. "How dare you say such a thing," she flashed at him.

"For the same reason that you dared to say the American history is full of lies; because it's true. All histories give a one-sided report of things."

I looked from one to the other of them uneasily. Ned's fair face was quiet and composed, but his grey eyes were flashing fire. Pauline beat a large, substantially shod foot excitedly on the floor. Her dark somber face was flushed from neck to brow.

"You ought to be put in jail for saying things like that," she stammered in the excess of her agitation.

"No matter whether it is true or not," Ned said. "That's the way with you tories; you're always wanting to put somebody in jail—as if that proved anything."

"But it isn't true," Pauline declared.

Ned was provokingly cool. "How do you know?" he asked quietly.

"Because it isn't."

"That's a fine reason," he sneered.

Pauline threw up her head. "I suppose you know better than the man who wrote the history, and the Board of Education, and all the teachers," she said crushingly.

The other students who had been idling about the room now gathered around to listen to the quarrel.

"I wouldn't accept the word of any Board of Education or a million teachers," Ned said. "I'd read both sides of the question myself, and form my own conclusions. My father says that if the histories were any good they would give us translations from the leading historians in every country on international events and leave us to judge for ourselves as to the facts."

"Your father is—"

We never heard what Ned's father was, for at that moment Mr. Magrath entered the room.

"What's all this noise about?" he demanded abruptly.

Silence fell upon us. Pauline always fought in the open. She was no tattle tale, but Minnie Forsyth spoke up. "Ned and Pauline were quarrelling because Ned said the English history was full of lies and Pauline said it wasn't."

Magrath turned to Pauline. "Is that true?" he demanded, his squatty figure trembling with passion and his thick neck scarlet.

Pauline shoved a pencil up and down between her long fingers in silence. In her rage she had threatened Ned with jail, but when it came to the test she was unwilling, much as she disliked him, to reveal his shortcoming to the super-patriot Magrath.

"Is this true, Pauline?" Magrath repeated.

"Yes, sir," Pauline answered, "but—but I don't think he meant it," she added generously.

"Yes, I did." Ned said quietly.

"Magrath turned pale. "Ned," he thundered, "take your books and go home. You're expelled."

Ned did not move.

"Did you hear me?" Magrath shouted.

"Certainly," Ned answered.

"Then why don't you obey me?"

"Because you have no authority to expel me from the school," Ned replied. It was uncanny the instinct Ned and his father had for law. They always knew to a nicety how far authority could go.

Magrath swallowed quickly. Then he turned on his heel and went to the desk. When he came back he carried an ugly black strap in his hand.

"There is something I have the authority to do." He hissed. "I can give you a good thrashing for dishonouring our country, you young American upstart."

I never saw Ned so cool and dignified as he was that

afternoon. He looked Magrath straight in the eye. "Put that thing down," he said in a quiet, powerful tone, "you can't prove with that thing that the English history is true."

Magrath wavered. I have no doubt that he was restrained partly by Ned's supple young muscles; partly by the fear that Tom Grant would go to law with him, for Tom Grant could plead a case so wittily and persuasively before a jury that everyone avoided meeting him in court.

At any rate he hesitated. The he threw back his shoulders and laughed. It was not a very good laugh, but it served as a back paddle in the argument.

"Very well, my smart young Socialist, I'll leave it to the trustees to decide whether you're to be allowed to contaminate the minds of the other students by making seditious speeches," and away he strutted and replaced the strap in his desk.

Ned took his seat, the object of the cold glances of all his associates. He turned to me. I looked down at my book. I admired Ned, and nearly always agreed with him, but being a coward, I felt sometimes that I did not like to be associated with him in the minds of my friends.

The moment it had happened I was ashamed, and tried to catch his eye, but he did not glance my way until about four o'clock, when he gave me a cold, hard look. I felt like one of those shrivelled little peas at the end of a pod.

He stalked off by himself when school was over, and left me to walk home alone, even though he knew Barry was at home sick, and Jean was spending the night in town with May.

When I reached home mother was sewing in a low rocker by the south kitchen window, and on the white oil cloth covered table there was ranged a quantity of fragrant yellow loaves of bread.

"There's a pan of buns there, Aleta," she said, glancing up as I came back from carrying my books into the dining-room.

I helped myself to a bun and spread it with yellow butter. Then I brought a stool and sat down beside mother's knee and told her about the quarrel between Ned and Pauline.

"What do you think, mother?" I asked.

She was holding the needle between her teeth while she took a new thread. "I don't know," she mumbled.

Then she took the needle from her mouth, licked the end of the thread, and holding them at arm's length brought them together.

To my surprise she continued. "I don't know but Ned was right. It seems to me very likely that histories are prejudiced. They may not say what is actually untrue, but they perhaps give a colour or implication to events that is not warranted, in order to make our country seem more perfect than it is."

Then I told her about having refused to look at Ned and how mean I felt.

Mother put down her sewing and patted my red brown head gently. "I'll tell you what you had better do, Aleta," she said after a little. "Put some of those buns in a bag and take them down to Ned and his father for super, and tell Ned you're sorry."

I jumped up with alacrity. "And you might take along

a bottle of that maple syrup," she called, when I was in the pantry hunting up a bag.

Father always grumbled that mother would give away everything we had, and certainly nearly half this consignment of maple syrup from Uncle Frank's farm in Ontario had gone in this way.

I went to the door. At the step I turned and looked at mother. Her round face, with its three-tier chin, was clearly outlined against the dark green foliage of the geraniums, and the sunlight, checkered by the leaves, fell across her sloping lap on to the grey-painted floor.

I went back and set my parcel on the table. Mother turned in surprise: "Did you forget something, Aleta?" she asked.

"Yes," I said smiling, and I put my hands on either side of her face and kissed her forehead. She looked both pleased and abashed. That evening I found she had made one of my favourite dishes, a baked custard for my supper.

I remember with a singular distinctness every detail of that walk to the Grant's. It was May; that is to say it was intoxicating. There is a secret urge in Spring everywhere. Even in languid humid climes it is the season of matings and revolutions. But Spring in the north! Air like champagne; a deluge of sunlight pouring down from cloudless blue skies; life bursting forth everywhere with an instinctive knowledge of the need for speed if it is to run its course and reproduce its kind before the early autumn frost overtakes it. It is life on the gallop to out-distance death. One stands in awe before the spectacle of this almost indecent hurry to survive.

As I followed the footpath along the barbed wire fence, which enclosed the pasture field, I thought with deep disgust of what had happened at school. Why couldn't I follow straight and swiftly my own opinions as the yellow buttercups at my feet went without self-consciousness to their goal? Why did I find myself apologetic when I did not agree with the majority? When I was given a mind that questioned everything, why was I not given a spirit that feared nothing? Since minds came into being that questioned things it seemed the world needed that kind of mind. Then why be ashamed of it? So I reasoned fruitlessly, for the wings of my soul had been clipped in my infancy. I had lost the power to fly while retaining the will to rise above the clouds of bigotry and prejudice.

*　　*　　*　　*　　*

The yard about the Grant's cottage was alive with high-stepping speckled Plymouth Rock hens, scratching backward, now and again, and pecking about daintily. One was even reconnoitring the kitchen through the partly open door.

The bright sunshine in the room increased the dreariness of its aspect. The greasy stove had a pot of porridge on the back. Pans were set out on chairs around the room, and the table was full of dirty dishes.

I rolled up my sleeves and set to work to make a fire. Then I began to wash up the dishes, expecting every moment that Ned would come in, but I had finished them, and swept and mopped the floor, and still there was no sign of Ned.

I was determined to see him and make it up, so I began to get supper. I had just finished setting the table when I heard his step at the door.

He stopped short when he saw me. "Hello, Aleta," he exclaimed in surprise.

It was my turn to be amazed. "Then you're not angry with me?" I asked shyly.

Ned twisted his cap in his hands. "I was at first," he admitted, "but afterward when I thought it over I saw that you had not been thinking about the matter of the histories in the way I had. You couldn't be expected to see it at once."

I was silent while a struggle went on inside. At last I spoke. "I hate to tell you, Ned," I said, "but it wasn't because I minded about the history that I didn't look at you." I picked up the knife and made little trails on the read damask cloth with it. "Just for a minute I—I—was ashamed," I confessed with chagrin.

Ned was silent.

Without raising my eyes I went on. "You won't understand. You're fearless. You don't mind what people think of you. But I do; I don't like being against people."

Still Ned was silent.

I looked up and saw him smiling. "I know," he said, "I've sometimes been ashamed of dad and of his being a Socialist."

"And your dad such a dear old man," I exclaimed, in a shocked voice.

Then we both laughed.

"We're in the same boat, Aleta," Ned said, "we'll always be against the popular side, so we may as well make up our minds to stand by each other."

He came close up to me, slipped his arm about my shoulders and looked down into my eyes with a queer expression.

I was startled. I looked Ned over with a new vision, from his boots to his smoothly parted silkily dark hair. His upper lip was blue. He had begun to shave. Ned was a man.

I looked down and giggled. It had flashed upon me all at once that I was a woman.

Ned closed his short-fingered, work-roughened hand over mine.

A great scraping was heard at the door. It was Ned's father come home from work. We blushed and sprang apart.

That night when I was going to bed I spent a long time sitting before my mirror. The person reflected there was not very satisfactory: short, stubby, a round sallow face with irregular features, and tanned. But there was my hair, long silky curls of red brown clustering about my head, and my dark brown eyes, which some people told me were beautiful. I brushed my hair until it crackled and stood out about my head in a shining cloud.

The next morning as I was helping mother get the breakfast, I said: "Do you know anything that will take off tan?"

Mother looked at me long and hard, almost resentfully, I thought.

"Buttermilk," she answered shortly.

*   *   *   *   *

They expelled Ned from school, thereby proving the accuracy of the English history, and his father planned to send him, for the balance of the term, to Winnipeg, where he meant to enter law school in the autumn anyway.

Ned came the evening before he left to say good-bye to us. He stayed only a little while. Father and Jean had never been particularly friendly to him, but even mother was a little cool, which I thought queer, since she had said she thought Ned was probably right.

But Barry brought him his greatest treasure, a knife with a corkscrew, several broken blades and a good one. He put it diffidently into Ned's hand.

"What's this?" Ned asked quickly.

Barry blushed and rubbed his close-cropped head up and down against Ned's arm. "It's for you," he answered proudly.

"Why thanks old man, that's awfully good of you, but I think you'll be needing it more than I will and you'd better keep it."

Barry took it quietly and slipped it into the back pocket of his funny little overalls.

I frowned. I knew that Ned's motive was kindly, for he knew how much Barry prized the knife, but the refusal of the gift seemed indelicate.

When Ned had said his farewells and I walked out with him to the gate, he said, "Wasn't it nice of the kid to offer me his knife? But of course I couldn't take it, he's so stuck on it himself."

"I think you made a mistake, Ned," I objected.

"Do you think so, Aleta?" he asked quickly. "I'm sorry if I've annoyed you. I seem to have got it wrong all round.

I suppose there are lots of things a fellow doesn't get on to when he grows up without a mother or sisters."

Ned was a very little boy at that moment and very sorry for himself, but there was something infinitely appealing about him. I glimpsed faintly what it meant for a boy to start out in the world without any woman to pet him and fuss over him.

So I held out both my hands. "Haven't I been almost as good as a sister to you, Ned?"

He took my hands in his and looked at me with the expression his face had worn the week before.

"Better," he said decidedly. "I'm awfully glad you're not my sister."

"Why?" I asked, provocatively.

"Will you kiss me, Aleta?" He demanded, suddenly.

I drew my hands away and shook my head. I wanted to kiss him, too, but something held me back. The puritanical may be inclined to put it down to maidenly modesty, but I think myself it was prudishness.

*   *   *   *   *

When I was sitting brushing my hair that night, Barry came in in his nighty. I saw that he carried in his hand the rejected gift.

"I guess it's not much good of a knife," he suggested, anxiously, disillusion dimming the smiling brightness of his dear blue eyes.

I held open my arms. "Come here, sonny," I said.

When he had come and cuddled against me, I said: "Did you think Ned didn't like your knife, Barry?"

Barry turned his back to me and dug his little pink toes into the rag carpet. "Uh-huh."

"You were wrong then, for Ned told me outside that he didn't take it because he knew you liked it so much."

"Then you think it's a good knife."

"Of course."

"Would you like to have it?"

"Would I like the pot of gold at the end of the rainbow?"

Barry clapped his hands jubilantly. "Then I'll give it to you."

After a thoughtful pause he suggested, "I suppose you wouldn't mind lending it to me now and again?"

"Not a bit," I agreed readily. "I'll leave it on this table and we can both use it."

So I did, and often it disappeared, but was always returned in the evening. Sometimes, to this day, when I put my hand down to the bottom of a certain old workbox it touches that knife, and my heart goes still, and a black cloud settles down upon my spirit.

CHAPTER IX.
The Storm Wind Again.

It was a winter night; not unlike the one on which Barry came into the world. Our house trembled and creaked as the north wind, charged with snow, came roaring down the road allowance and broke, with an impotent shriek, against the rattling windows.

But this time there was no long wait for the doctor. He had been in the house since morning. Barry lay very still on the bed, except for the heavy breathing of pneumonia. Mostly he lay in a stupor, but whenever he grew brighter he asked for mother and me, so we stayed near at hand.

The still excitement of a very serious sickness makes a queer halting place in one's experience. All the usual things give place to the unusual. That day we spoke with hushed voices, and walked softly even in the kitchen, where we could not possibly have disturbed Barry.

Mother was dark about the eyes and quiet; father was silent, and Jean pale. As for me something had happened that morning that had completely upset me. Perhaps that day would have been less awful if I had shared it with the others. I tried several times, but my lips refused to do my bidding.

I had been left alone with Barry for a few minutes when he roused up and asked for some water. I put my arm around him and raised him up, for he was very weak. As I laid him back on the pillow he whispered something.

"What is it Barry?" I asked.

He repeated it, and this time I caught the words, "Does it hurt much to die?"

"No," I answered, my voice trembling, "but you're not going to die." Then I was seized into a panic, and repeated wildly, "You're not going to die; you're not going to die. You wouldn't leave Aleta, would you, Barry?"

He was sinking again into a stupor, but I think he answered "No."

Mother came in just then with a bottle of medicine in her hand. "Mother," I said, drawing in a long sobbing breath. She laid a plump hand on my arm, "What is it dear?" she asked anxiously.

I shook my head, went to the window, and stood looking through a clear spot at the top of a thickly frosted pane upon the flat white desolation, which spread out unbroken to meet the distant cold sky.

What had made the child think of death, I questioned, and could find no answer. Nobody would have spoken to him about it. Was it intuition? Was it premonition? I did not weep, but the landscape seemed completely blotted out. I saw before me, instead of the brilliant winter world, a long, dark avenue, where neither the sun, nor the moon nor the stars did shine, and where there was only a dim grey gate at the end leading into the garden of death. That was life as it looked without Barry.

The doctor came at eleven. He took Barry's temperature, felt his pulse, and shook his head.

"I believe the crisis will come sometime today or this

evening," he replied, when questioned, and announced his intention of staying.

I had not noticed until that day that Jean was a woman. It came to me when I saw the doctor, who was young and single, give her an admiring glance, which passed her by unnoticed. She was quite unconscious of his approval, as her thoughts were all with her little brother battling for his life upstairs.

She was a great comfort to everyone at that time. A born housekeeper, she took things into her own hands; tidied the house, as usual, prepared tempting hot meals, and coaxed us one after another to eat them. It is a blessed thing in the house of sickness to have someone about who translates sorrow into service.

As for me, I hardly know how I spent that day. It seems to me I moved about in a dark shadow made deeper by the storm that overspread the sky in the late afternoon, and that before me there moved always that pathetic little question, "Does it hurt much to die?"

When night settled in, and the storm, grown to a blizzard, roared and shrieked about the house, a superstitious fear took possession of me. Barry had come into the world in a blizzard. Had the storm wind come back for him?

The hours crept away, and as the evening wore on, Dr. Graham stayed continuously at Barry's side, looking anxious and feeling his pulse very frequently.

About ten o'clock he laid the little hand back on the bed and looked at us strangely.

*   *   *   *   *

The sun streaming in through the thickly frosted window and turning it into a sheet of glittering diamonds, looked cheerful. I sat up in bed briskly. I had had an awful dream. It had been that Barry was gone. A terrible dream.

I caught my breath suddenly. Did I remember, or was it a nightmare, the little hand being laid back on the bed, and that I walked the floor for the rest of the night, and all the next day tearless and silent, until they had sent for the doctor, who had given me a glass of milk with a queer taste.

I remembered.

After that for a long time I beat the wings of my will, which would not have it so, against the absolute fact that it was so. What seemed hours later I put on my clothes and crept downstairs. As I was passing the parlour door I saw something white standing by the window. I stopped short; went on again; turned back and drew near to that small white box. Barry's face, waxy and still, smiled up at me. His question was answered. It does not hurt to die— only to live.

I knelt down beside that little white coffin, laid my head on it and wept. Presently I felt two arms slipped about me, and my head was gently moved from the hard coffin to a friendly shoulder. I looked up into Pauline's kind, brown, eyes. She did not tell me, as Minnie Forsyth had tried to do the day before, that Barry was better dead—poor comfort that when the heart was crying out for him. We wept quietly together, and the memory of that morning beside Barry's coffin keeps Pauline from quite hating me now, and me from hating her. We would not have believed then that the day would come when we would look the other way when we met on the street.

Everybody went out to the graveyard, and when we came back the chairs were all in rows, as they had been for the service; the fire was out, and some of the men who had come to the funeral had missed the ashpan of the kitchen stove and spat on the floor around it. In this dreary house, and on that cold winter day, I started life all over again at sixteen without Barry.

CHAPTER X.
Agnosticism.

When Ned came home from Winnipeg the next June we made a great discovery. It was on a Sunday evening after church. All we girls walked out of the service with downcast eyes, in spite of which we managed to see the youths who detached themselves from their fellows, and proudly yet nervously approached us with uplifted hats.

Ned joined us, and after the custom of the village we turned to stroll down the most densely maple shaded street, for the long northern summer evening has only well begun at eight o'clock.

When we had adjusted our pace to that of the couples fore and aft so as to be out of earshot of both, Ned turned to me and asked, "What do you think of Christianity, Aleta?"

"I think it is perhaps the purest system of morals the world has yet evolved," I answered patly, greatly to his surprise and my own, for I was hardly conscious that I had been thinking about Christianity at all.

Then we had what the Indians would call a pow-wow over our unbelief. We went step by step along that path that had led us to our present conclusions, and to our great delight found them to be identical. In half an hour we had disposed of the inspiration of the Bible, the Divinity of Christ, and put a big blue question mark over the immortality of the soul. We felt that we had done a good night's work and went home in a highly elated mood.

I said good-night to Ned and went in past Jean and Dr. Graham, who were standing by the gate talking. An hour or two later I glanced out of the window and saw them kissing in the moonlight. I was disgusted.

When Jean mentioned Dr. Graham the next day I said: "I think he is horribly soft and very homely."

Jean flushed angrily. "He's much better looking than Ned, at any rate," she declared.

"Well, I don't think I ever said Ned was good looking, did I?" was my reply and Jean was baffled.

After that I was mean enough never to miss a chance of saying something unpleasant about Dr. Graham, for I was furious at the idea that Jean might get married and I would be shut out from her life.

*　　*　　*　　*　　*

The next Sunday night I declined to go to church. "Why not?" mother asked.

I was on the point of telling her how foolish it all was, but something held me back. I could blast anybody's faith but my mother's. Insufferable little egoist that I was to suppose that the walls of my mother's faith, which had stood through all the storms of life, would fall at one puny blast from my trumpet. But I really thought I was sparing her a great disillusionment by answering merely that I was tired.

Ned came over later and we sat on the verandah steps and wordily patronised people who attended churches.

Ned was sitting in the sunlight, and I where the shadows of the house fell over my white muslin dress and black Oxford shoes. In one of the pauses of the conversation I studied him thoughtfully. His strong, medium-sized figure and filled out wonderfully during the past year, and since he had been to Winnipeg he was always clean and neatly dressed.

My concentrated gaze made him turn his rugged face towards me, and he smiled revealing a row of large white teeth.

"It's wonderful how well we suit each other, isn't it Aleta?" he asked, sidling over nearer me on the steps.

I sidled a little away, I couldn't just say why. But he kept coming closer. He took my hand and pressed it and looked at me with far other thoughts than of religion shining in his eyes. I squirmed and drew my hand away, for the woman in me was still sound asleep, and that look of the man seeking his mate, which I saw in Ned's eyes, made me uncomfortable.

"Don't you like me, Aleta?" he questioned.

"Why yes," I answered, "but we're too young for that. I want to do ever so many things before—" I broke off abruptly and studied the clear horizon flushed by the sunset.

"What's the use of starting a lot of things and having to give them up when you get married?" Ned objected.

"Maybe I wouldn't give them up," I said.

"You'd have to," he returned flatly.

I frowned. I was very immature, and had thought very little about the marriage relationship, but this speech of Ned's grated unpleasantly upon me.

CHAPTER XI.
McNair.

It was twelve years later that I was riding home to Winnipeg, one winter afternoon, on a train that crept slowly over the creaking frosty rails. From my chair in the parlour car I watched the smooth fields of snow slip past the train windows, the while I enlarged upon the points I had not made in an address I had delivered upon woman suffrage in an outlying village the evening before.

While I was adding wit and grace retrospectively to a speech which had been dull enough in reality, the train slowed down with a harsh grinding sound, jerked us nearly out of our seats, and stopped.

A huge man unfolded himself from the seat next mine, rose up to a prodigious height and breadth; shook his brown tweed trousers down over his tan boots; walked with a slow, echoless tread to the door, and went out.

When he returned he was carrying in his hand one of the city papers. He spread it out on his knee and we began to read it. I had covered the headings of the big murder trial, and was into the latest political scandal when he turned over.

He insists to this day that I gave a sharp exclamation of annoyance, which is, of course, absurd. I did nothing of the kind, but however that may be he looked up, our eyes met and we smiled.

"Did I turn too soon?" he asked mildly, but with a twinkle in his eye.

"Just three more lines," I said laughing, and he turned back and let me see them. So we shared the paper between us, and from that we went on to talk of books, plays and the like, and he dug about in his capacious pockets and brought out several little scrap books with poems and snatches of philosophy. While I read them he watched me with eager grey eyes, which in their boyishness belied his otherwise mature appearance. He seemed oddly anxious that I should not think them foolish.

On one of these excursions into an inside pocket he brought out a photograph with the book he was after, hesitated a moment, then handed it to me with a smile. "That's my boy Colin," he said pridefully, and watched my face harder than ever for approval.

My heart sank. It was a shock to me to find that the stranger was married.

"He's a nice boy," I said coldly, "but he doesn't look much like you."

As if in answer to my thoughts the stranger explained quickly, "I am only his guardian, but I could not think more of him if he were my own son."

"He's a manly looking little chap," I amended cordially, and I smiled at the photograph of a grave little lad of about thirteen years.

The stranger went on to explain about him. "His mother died when he was born, and his father when he was three, and when his father, who was my dearest friend, was dying he sent for me and said, 'McNair, I'm going to leave Colin to you, to raise like your own son.'

"That was back in Scotland," he concluded. "I supposed you guessed I was a Scotchman."

I smiled. "Guessed?" And the man had been filling the car with burrs ever since he had begun to speak.

But what had I heard about some McNair lately? Memory came in a flash. "Would you be the Mr. McNair who has come up from the East to edit the Rural Review?" I asked.

"The same," he admitted, surprised.

"Then you and I are sworn enemies. I'm on the Country Register."

Memory came to his aid also. "You wouldn't be Miss Aleta Dey?" he suggested, hesitatingly, as one unwilling to accuse anybody unjustly.

I nodded assent, and I never saw a more disappointed looking man. "Then you're a suffragette."

"Gist," I corrected, gently but firmly.

He paid no attention to the distinction, which was swallowed up in the general disaster, but sat silently glowering into the dusk, his face drawn down into deep haggard lines as he chewed away at the amber stem of his unlighted pipe.

At last he turned to me, and his face brightened with a most engaging smile. "Anyway, you've good notions about books," he said, dwelling charitably upon my one redeeming quality. "Let's go and have a bite to eat, and by that time we'll be in the city," and he stuffed the pipe in his pocket and led the way to the dining car.

When we parted at the station he put out his big hand and I laid my wee one in it, and I cannot tell you how it happened, but a thrill, such as I had never experienced in my life before, passed up my right arm and down my left side, and I knew, without looking at the great man, who was standing there holding my hand as if it was a parcel I had given him for keeps, that he felt the thrill, too.

"I'd be glad to have the pleasure of your acquaintance, if I may," he was saying in his quaint old-fashioned manner.

I took my hand away at last, being driven to it by a sense of decency, and searched in my handbag for a card, which I gave him.

"You may call on me some evening at that address, if you care to," I said. And so we parted.

Had my father been alive he would have been scandalized to see me go home and hurry straight to the rouge pot, which was requisitioned only on such state occasions as came when I was all tired out and looking my worst. I applied unsparingly, and then dabbed myself with powder until even mother would have been shocked if she had been present, which luckily she was not, having gone, after father's death, to help nurse the babies of Jean and Dr. Graham, who were married and settled in Souris River, next door to May Ransome and her husband.

I looked at myself critically in the glass. It was a great improvement on Nature's handiwork, but it wouldn't do. The improvement was too obvious. So I went out to Mrs. Fleming's sink and scrubbed my face clean of the mess. When I came back to my parlour bedroom I looked my wardrobe over carefully and found I had not a decent dress to put on. I decided to get myself a new one the very next day, which I did.

CHAPTER XII.
A Tilt About Socialism.

When I was considering the new dress, Pauline hailed me from the aisle and hastened to join me. She was a tall young woman now, and head of the children's department of the public library.

"Isn't this luck?" she exclaimed, "Something's burst in the steam plant, so we are closed up, and I was looking for somebody to play with. Let's go ... and ... have .... some ..... tea."

The last sentence died out, as I have tried to indicate, when her glance fell upon the dresses the clerk had ranged before me.

"Why, Aleta," she exclaimed, "you're not buying a summer dress at this season of the year, are you?"

I did not want to explain to Pauline that there are occasions, even during the cold weather, when such a dress is useful, especially if light colours are more becoming to one than dark; for example, when one is receiving a caller informally in the evening.

But I merely said, "It's the last day of February, Pauline."

"Yes; but, my dear, you'll not get any wear out of a dress like that before June, and then they will be less expensive. Come and look at these silks."

I had great respect for Pauline's opinion about clothes,

for she is twice as clever as I in the matter of dress, so I followed her. She tried to foist a sober blue and black thing upon me, but I would have none of it, and stood out for a warm burgundy, which Pauline thought was too dear, but as I was paying for it I had my way. And the next day I went back and bought the pink muslin, too, though I would not like Pauline to find that out. She thinks I do not save enough.

When we had completed the purchase of the taffeta dress, Pauline and I hunted up one of those pretty little tea rooms, which make Winnipeg a decent place in which to live.

"Well, how did you get along at your meeting?" she asked, as she finished writing the order on the tiny pad.

"I made a great speech on the train coming home," I admitted, with a laugh.

Pauline laughed, too, as she threw aside her furs. She was an ardent suffragist. In our outlook upon public life that was the one point of contact between us.

"There were a couple of Socialists there who got up and fired questions at me about the capitalist system, which I was not in a position to answer," I said.

"They make me sick," Pauline declared, "with their everlasting 'Capitalist System' and 'Class conscious workers.' A lot of ignorant beggars, too lazy to get out and earn a decent living for themselves, so they want to grab what honest people make."

"There's more to Socialism than that, Pauline," I objected. "Some of those people are poor because they have been so weakened by malnutrition in their youth, and so hampered by the lack of an education that they haven't a chance in the struggle for existence."

"I don't believe it," Pauline said, flatly.

"Have you no imagination," I asked indignantly, "that you seem incapable of sympathising with any injustice except this matter of woman suffrage, which touches you personally. Do you intend to go through life saying, 'I don't believe it' about everything it would make you uncomfortable to face?'

Pauline's face took on that patronising, supercilious expression, which always made Ned want to strangle her, and she said, "Don't give me one of Ned's lectures secondhand, Aleta. It's bad enough to have to endure the first edition when one can't escape it."

Perhaps it as Pauline's commanding physical presence which enabled her to seem to put me completely in the wrong, when the only answer she could make to any facts I offered for her consideration was, "I don't believe it."

She was the most perfect type I have ever known of established authority, frequently benevolent, always unimaginative, and so sure of herself that if such a thing as a dispute between herself and God were possible she would know that God was mistaken.

I, on the other hand, had often the unpleasant aggressiveness of timidity; the self-assertion which frequently arises from being driven by an unknown urge to defy authority of which one stands in awe.

I have always felt that I owe that fear of authority to my stern upbringing, to my father's cruel chastisements in particular, and I have never conquered my resentment of it. So when my father died I shed no tears. It would have been black hypocrisy to weep for the man who whipped my spirit into servility.

I suppose there is no unpardonable sin, but if there were I am sure it would be this, for authority so to en-chain a man's soul with fear that he loses the power "to draw the Thing as he sees it, for the God of the Things as they are."

CHAPTER XIII.
A Visitor.

It was a week later that I was called to the telephone, and a deep, rich voice said over the wire, "This is McNair speaking."

I beamed upon that telephone and said, "Oh, yes, Mr. McNair."

"I was thinking that if you were going to be disengaged this evening I would call upon you," he continued.

I cancelled in intention a walk I had planned to take, and assured him I was quite free and would be delighted to see him.

As I went home in the sharp frosty darkness I gathered up tasty things for refreshments on the way, and arrived there I hunted out a pair of white silk stockings, and swept and dusted the room till it shone, and laid a fire in the grate, and bathed and put on my finest and daintiest things.

After dinner, of which Mrs. Fleming complained that I ate hardly a mouthful, I slipped into my own room and donned the white silk stockings and my white kid pumps, and lastly the delicate rose muslin frock which set off my dark hair and complexion to the best possible advantage.

At last I sat down to wait and looked about the room with a feeling of genuine satisfaction. Little by little I had eliminated Mrs. Fleming from the place. At the last house cleaning I had persuaded her to let me have a warm buff kalsomine on the walls instead of the brightly medallioned paper she had in mind, and a plain brown grass rug in exchange for the bright green leaves and pink flowers of the tapestry, which fitted the measure of her purse. And one by one I had carried up the back bedroom the ugly plush-covered chairs and substituted for them cretonned-cushioned rockers and easy chairs of willow.

So that to-night as I looked about the room, fragrant with pots of crocus, and blue, pink, and heliotrope hyacinths, which filled the sills of the windows at the side of the room, and overflowed on to the top of the bookcase and table, I had a feeling of genuine pride in this little place, which was all I had of home in the world.

I rose and moved the tea table up beside the fire, and took the copper tray, filled with dull green dishes from the top of the bookcase and set it on the table. Then I stood back to admire the effect. At that moment the bell rang. I touched a match to the firewood in the grate and hurried to the door.

There was McNair, bigger than I had remembered him. Again my little palm was laid against his huge one, and again a thrill went through me as he closed his fingers over mine.

He stooped his head to enter the doorway of my room, and looked about him in pleased surprise. "You're very cosy here, aren't you?" he remarked, and I cannot say how gratified I was that he thought my place pretty.

I watched him, smiling to myself, as he let himself down circumspectly into the biggest and strongest of my chairs, which at that was a poor fit for him.

As it groaned under his weight he gave me an appre-
hensive look, and inquired anxiously, "Do you think it
will hold?"

I expressed my confidence in the furniture and he
leaned back in the chair; stretched his long legs out to the
fire; put his hand instinctively into the pocket of his coat,
and brought it quickly away empty, remembering his man-
ners in the nick of time.

"Wouldn't you like to smoke?" I asked, rightly inter-
preting the action.

He beamed on me, drew out his pipe and filled it, drib-
bling the tobacco carelessly on the rug, as a man is apt to
do when he has been a bachelor for too long, and had
women paid to run around after him and keep silent about
the trouble he makes.

He puffed hard at his pipe for a few seconds; took it
from his mouth; watched the smoke curl slowly
ceilingward. Then he turned to me with that winning
smile of his, "You're sure you don't mind?" he asked.

"Not in the least," I lied cheerfully. As a matter of fact
tobacco smoke does not agree with me very well, giving
me a headache if taken in too large quantities, but I
wouldn't have had him know that for any consideration.
I wanted him to like me, and I knew that if it were a choice
between that pipe and me I wouldn't have a chance in the
world. The lies we women tell at such times! But God
knows we have to or we would never get ourselves mates,
so He overlooks it.

And now, being thoroughly comfortable, McNair
turned to me, and I knew that he was aware that I was
looking very well in my rose gown, and very likely he was

thinking what a sensible little woman I was to buy such simple dainty things. I could have told him, if I'd had a mind to, that the more simple a woman's clothes look the harder her husband is going to have to work to pay for them, but as The Preacher says, "He that increaseth knowledge increaseth sorrow."

I had planned before he came that I would talk to McNair about sensible things like politics (at that time I believed politics to be a rational subject) and let him see how intelligent I was, so I was amazed to hear myself saying, "How do you like my new dress?"

It was all wrong. I did not want McNair to know it was a new dress, in the first place, lest he should think I had bought it on his account, which I had, and in the second because it was frivolous. But from the moment we met in the train McNair and I fitted together so comfortably that all the proprieties of a new acquaintanceship fell away from us naturally.

He looked surprised and oddly pleased at the question.

"I was just thinking what a pretty gown it is," he answered gravely, "though I don't know much about women's things. I was left an orphan when I was a little shaver and went to work young. About all the education I ever got was at night school, and through reading books I picked up by myself."

With this glimpse of his past I began to understand the secret of McNair's charm as well as his shy diffidence about the queer medley of things he liked, and his boyish eagerness to share them with someone.

"And since I've grown up…" McNair began again, paused, drew his mouth down gloomily at the corners, and stared silently into the fire. It struck me that he had one of the saddest faces I had ever seen.

At last he raised his head and looked at me with a deep melancholy in his gentle grey eyes. "I may be obliged to explain to you some day why I have had so little to do with women since I have grown up," he said. "Perhaps I ought to do so now, but I don't see that it would do any good."

"Mr. McNair," I returned, in answer to the implied question of his tone, "there is nothing about you which I am not willing to take on trust."

He looked exceedingly pleased, and grateful. "That is very good of you," he said, in a deep rich voice.

I could not see that it was, since it seemed to me that the whole atmosphere of the man breathed a clean, wholesome outlook upon life. That is still my opinion, though I now know the two things he had in mind when he asked the question.

He now reached down into his pocket and brought out one of the old classics and read me a passage from it, and that started an argument, and then McNair, being Scotch, was in his element. We chased each other up hill and down dale with words, and whenever I pursued him too hotly he would put his fingers together thoughtfully, look at me with a smile and say, "I wonder."

In which circumstances there was nothing to be done but smile back, and maybe give him another cup of tea or a sandwich, which last he would wave in my face by way of emphasizing a point.

CHAPTER XIV.
Ned Again.

On a certain unlucky night Ned met McNair at my room. Several times they had missed each other by an hour or two, but at last they came together. And they clashed immediately. An election was imminent and Ned was working night and day for an independent candidate, while McNair was throwing all his influence on the side of the Conservatives. After I had introduced them there was a pause for a moment before Ned turned to me with the question:

"Did you see that article about Fraser in this morning's 'Times'?"

As it happened I had not seen it.

McNair chuckled. "I think that was the wittiest bit of writing I have seen in a long time," he declared. "I wonder who did it?"

I looked anxiously at Ned's dark frowning face as he glared with dilating nostrils at McNair.

When he spoke his voice trembled with suppressed temper. "You thought it witty, did you? I thought it the most contemptible example of mud-slinging we've had in the campaign, and I can't say any worse of it than that."

So they began a sharply contested battle on the political situation, Ned appealing to me several times for support, which I gave unequivocally. It seemed to me that no one but an intense partisan would support the side McNair was advocating, and I did not hesitate to say so. It is true I loved McNair and I wanted him to love me, but I could not pretend to be other than I was to gain that end.

I noticed that the first time Ned called me Aleta, McNair looked quickly from him to me, and from that time forward he was more sarcastic in his arguments than I had ever known him to be. Altogether it was a most unpleasant hour before McNair, who had an engagement at the office, rose to leave.

I went to the outside door with him, and when I gave him my hand to say good-night he pressed it very gently, releasing it with a caressing touch of each finger, which brought a flood of colour to my face.

When I returned to the room Ned exclaimed in a tone of deep disgust, "Did you ever see such a hopeless reactionary? How do you stand him?"

"We need some brakes on the wheel of progress, Ned," I apologised for McNair.

He yawned contemptuously behind his hand. "It's not much of a job, though, for a full-sized man. He might leave that to women."

"Why, Ned," I exclaimed indignantly, "I thought you were a feminist." Ned was a leading light in our suffrage organisation.

He had the grace to blush. "So I am," he protested quickly; "don't be cross, Aleta."

"But I am cross," I answered. "Theoretically you believe in the equality of the sexes, but practically you do not feel that we are equal any more than McNair does. If you had a wife you would bully her with the worst of them."

Ned was sitting stooped over, with his knees spread out and his hands clasped between them. At that he turned and gave me a straight look with his piercing grey eyes. "I wish you would give me a chance to prove that you are wrong in that, Aleta," he said quietly, but with a deep seriousness.

"Please don't—Ned," I stammered, twisting my handkerchief in my hands. "I—I don't want to hurt you again."

"All right," he replied, with a quick intake of his breath, "I'll just wait until you do learn to care for me."

He must have read something in my face, for he stopped short.

"Unless," he suggested, "unless you have learned to care for someone else?"

The colour mounted to my forehead, as I nervously smoothed the handkerchief on my lap.

"Is it McNair?"

The words fell upon the silence with such a queer hoarse sound that I turned anxiously to look at Ned. His face was blanched, and there was a drawn look about his lips.

Another wave of colour surged over my face as I nodded my head slowly.

After a long silence Ned cleared his throat and asked, "Do you know anything about this man's life, Aleta?"

"Very little," I answered, "and I am not willing to know any more than he is prepared to tell me himself."

I think that speech, more than anything I could have said, convinced Ned of my infatuation for McNair. He went away shortly, and from that time forward came to see me less often.

That night as I lay in bed I was filled with wonder at the criss-crosses of life. I agreed with Ned's opinions on most things, nearly everything, in fact, and I knew him to be one of the most upright men God ever made. A seer of visions, he went more than half way to meet progress, so that as a citizen he far out-shone McNair, but—but— well, I had never found myself measuring how far my head would come up supposing I stood within the circle of his arms, or trembling at the imagined pressure of his lips on mine. I have never stood in McNair's arms either, but if I had I know that my head would hardly have come to the level of his heart.

CHAPTER XV.
Colin Refuses To Come.

It happened that Mrs. Fleming, who was a widow and childless, had an invalid cousin, with whom she took tea every Sunday evening, and that left me alone to get tea for myself, so I arranged to have McNair come for this meal, and I asked him to bring the boy Colin along.

The first Sunday night he said the boy had a toothache, and the next a headache, and the third a toe so sore he could not get his boot on, and I knew by the way McNair told me of these disablements that he took them all in good faith.

"Why, McNair," I said the third night, "he doesn't want to come."

McNair opened his eyes very wide and drew his face down solemnly, "Do you think not?" he asked. "Why do you say that?"

"Because they are all my old Sunday school excuses," I laughed.

McNair frowned; put his table napkin on the cloth, squeezing it all in a bunch under his big hand, and rose from the table.

"Where are you going?" I asked, as he marched with that slow stately step of his out into the hall.

He did not answer, so I got up and ran after him and caught him just as he was going out of the door with his hat jammed down on his head.

"Where are you going?" I asked again, catching him by the coat and holding him.

"I'm going to fetch the young rascal. He'll not insult your hospitality like that."

"If you do I'll lock you both out when you come back," I threatened.

"Why?"

"Come indoors, so that the neighbours won't see me trying to keep you here against your will, and I'll tell you."

When we were seated I rested my chin in the palm of my hand and looked across that table at McNair, who with his stiff, lightish hair all awry was stirring his cup of tea violently.

"Don't you know you couldn't have brought Colin?" I asked. "No, you couldn't," I insisted, as he opened his mouth to protest. "You might have used your great physical force, or your power as his guardian to bring Colin's body, but his goodwill would have escaped you. That would likely have been turned to hatred towards me for having been, indirectly, the cause of this outrage against his personal liberty."

I told him of the cruel punishments to which I had been subjected as a child, and how I had learned from them that real power over the mind of anyone is in inverse ratio to the use of physical force. He listened sympathetically, for McNair is that rare member of the human species, a person who listens with enthusiasm.

"And so I don't want you to bring Colin by force," I concluded, "For I want your boy to love me."

As I said it I blushed and looked down and took up a

spoon from beside my plate and began to make lines on the cloth with it.

McNair was silent so long that I looked up, and was surprised to see him sitting in a tense attitude, sideways to the table, his right hand closed upon a crumpled napkin, his left clenched on his knee, and his face drawn down into deep haggard lines, while he stared out of the window with that sad expression I had often surprised in his eyes.

He must have felt my eyes upon him, for he turned to me with a wistful smile and said gently, "I was taking for granted that he wouldn't be able to help it when he came to know you."

Then indeed I blushed furiously, and waited breathlessly for him to say more. But he only took his pipe from his pocket, lit it and puffed gloomily into the twilight. However, as I went about the task of clearing up I felt that his eyes often followed me.

Before he went home that evening we had made a plan for capturing Colin. The next Sunday evening he was not to come to tea, but I would meet them on the street going to the restaurant for dinner, and be asked to join them.

They were to be coming up the north side of Portage Avenue, between Garry and Hargrave Streets at ten minutes to six.

"Mind you're not late," was McNair's parting injunction.

CHAPTER XVI.
Wooing Colin.

Sunday came, a bright April day, but raw. I watched the time carefully so that I should not have to wait long on the street and yet should not miss them.

And I walked slowly and then fast, and the jeweller's clock said ten to six and five to six, and still there was no sign of McNair and the boy. I had worn my spring coat, because it was more becoming than my fur one, and I was nearly perishing.

Suddenly I was hailed from across the street, and there was McNair beckoning to me. And he was alone.

"Woman," he exclaimed indignantly, when I had come within speaking distance, "don't you know the difference between the north and south side of the street?"

McNair was blue with cold, too, and very angry with me, but I had no time to think of that yet. "Where's Colin?" I asked, deeply disappointed that he was not there.

"I sent him back for a pocket handkerchief I did not want," McNair said, "and if you'll go around that corner, and down one block and back, I think we'll meet according to plan."

So it turned out all right in spite of my mistake and I met Colin.

When McNair said, "this is my boy Colin, of whom I've been speaking to you," I put out my hand and he touched his cap, and allowed me to hold a limp, cold, un-responsive fist for a fraction of a minute before he drew it away and thrust it into the pocket of his bloomer trousers.

As McNair asked me in his best imitation of an off-hand manner to have tea with them, I noticed a disappointed expression pass over the boy's face as if he had been counting on having McNair to himself this evening. Yet I was selfish enough to go.

At first I talked mostly to McNair, but afterwards I turned to the boy, a lad tall for his thirteen years, and with a dour Scotch face. I tried to discover what he liked, and experimented with boating, baseball and tennis, but he would merely answer 'yes' and 'no' to my questions and look down again at his plate.

At last I gave him up in despair, and, turning again to McNair, I began to speak of an historical pageant that was to be given the next week at the exhibition grounds, and of the aviator who was going to take part in it.

Colin put down his knife and leaned forward.

"Are you interested in aviation, Colin?" I asked, turning, to him quickly.

"A—a—little," he stammered, taken unawares.

"So am I," I said heartily. Then a great inspiration came to me.

"Colin," I suggested, "would you take me out to the exhibition grounds to see the flying? Mr. McNair can't go with me," I added, quickly to forestall the suggestion I saw trembling on his lips.

Even so he did not fully grasp the situation and was about to protest when I glared at him and he subsided into silence, while Colin awkwardly consented to be my squire.

"Why wouldn't you let me go to the show?" McNair asked when we had parted from Colin and were on our way to my place.

"Because people get acquainted in twos, not in threes," I replied, "and I want you to be good and leave me alone to woo your boy in my own way."

"Very well," he agreed quietly.

"And, McNair," I added, "you're to give the lad plenty of money to pay his way and mine, for I want him to feel he is taking care of me that day."

"Do you, indeed!" he exclaimed in a tone of assumed indignation. "You make nothing at all of ordering a man to stay at home and pay the bills."

He did not refer to the matter again until we were saying good-night at the gate, an hour later. As we shook hands he looked down at me with a twinkle in his eye and asked, "Must I make allowance for an ice-cream cone too?"

"Surely," I agreed, laughing.

He pressed my hand very gently: "I'm thinking you are wonderfully wise in the weaknesses of we men folk, and the way you exploit them is scandalous."

*   *   *   *   *

So Colin and I went to the pageant, and he paid my way everywhere, for McNair had been more than liberal. I could see that he was proud to be able to ask me to go into whatever booth took our fancy.

"Now, Miss Dey, let's go up to the grandstand and see the flying," he suggested, as we came away from having our fortunes told.

I agreed, and we watched, from the best of seats, the thrilling performance, and every little while Colin would exclaim, "Did you see that now, Miss Dey?"

When it was over, and some other phase of the pageant had begun, I rose and said to Colin, "Come along, laddie," and he came along but mutinously, looking very glum as we made our way down from the grandstand and along the fence.

When we were a little way out of the crowd I stopped and explained: "I've an appointment to interview the aviator, Colin, and I thought you might like to meet him."

Such a look of awed gladness flashed into his face that I was more than repaid for all the trouble it had cost me to make the arrangement. And, anyway, wasn't he McNair's boy, and didn't we have to be friends?

The aviator was a pleasant young chap, and finding that Colin asked intelligent questions he answered him man to man fashion, and allowed him to sit in the machine and showed him how it worked.

I think I never saw a boy so happy. All the way home his face wore a rapt expression, as if he found life too wonderful to be true. When he left me at my gate, and I thanked him for a delightful afternoon, he said, with boyish frankness, "Thank ye, too, Miss Dey, for introducing me to the flying man. Won't the kids at school be jealous, though?"

*   *   *   *   *

So the ice was broken and Colin came with McNair to tea the next Sunday night and all the Sunday nights that followed. He would take a book, throw himself into a chair, with his legs dangling over the arm, and read.

One Sunday evening McNair came solemnly in from the garden seat under the maple tree by the gate, and asked, "May I send the boy to help wash up?" He had helped me himself once, but he did it so badly that I ordered him off to his pipe.

"You may not," I answered firmly.

"I thought as much," he growled at me between puffs. "It's terrible the way you bully me, young woman, even about my own lad." And he marched slowly back, with his heavy echoless tread, to the garden seat, where I usually joined him when I had finished my work.

But it occurred to me that perhaps Colin felt left out, so this evening I went in to my sitting room, where he was draped loosely over the big stuffed chair I had bought since McNair became a regular visitor.

My heart was touched at the thought that this boy had never known any mothering, though, to be sure, the affection between him and McNair was the most beautiful thing I had ever seen in my life. Still they were both Scotch, poor things, and something told me the lad needed mothering. I perched on the arm of the chair and began to talk to him about "The Three Guardsmen," which he was reading. From that I went on to lay my hand on his head and run my fingers through his hair.

"What are you doing there?" he asked, turning his head back and looking up at me with his bright brown eyes.

The words sounded cross, but there was something in the tone which encouraged me to continue.

"I was pretending you were my little brother," I answered, and I told him about Barry.

There are few things more touching than the way a young person responds to a simple sincere confidence given without condescension.

"Gee, you must have felt awful bad when he died," he said, sympathetically, and leaned his head without reserve against my shoulder. I stooped and pressed my lips very gently to his forehead. From that moment I began to love Colin for his own sake, and not because he was McNair's laddie. He must have felt the difference, I imagine, for he permitted me after this to mother him in secret to my heart's content. The next Sunday night he came and offered to help me with the dishes, and we had long talks about things, not important enough to be set down here. Altogether we three were so happy that I might have known it could not last.

CHAPTER XVII.
The Quarrel.

McNair and I quarrelled. It happened this way. Our suffrage organisation had decided to have a parade to awaken a slothful public to the importance of our propaganda. I cannot convey any idea of how distasteful the thing was to me; of how I shrank from the unpleasant conspicuousness of walking down a street lined with spectators. We were to be dressed in white and to wear large orange sashes across our shoulders bearing the legend, "Votes for Women."

On a certain evening, a week before the parade, I was contemplating, with a feeling of nausea of which I was deeply ashamed, this outfit lying over the back of a chair, when McNair came in.

"What trumpery is this?" he inquired, superciliously, noticing it almost immediately, and grasping the significance of it as promptly.

I told him that it was my costume for the parade, and because I hated it so much and was so ashamed of myself for my self-consciousness, I was sharper and firmer than I had any need to be.

"You're not going to make a spectacle of yourself like that, are you?" he interrogated contemptuously.

"It all depends upon what one calls a spectacle," I retorted, beating my toe angrily upon the floor.

"I should certainly not permit my wife, if I had one, to carry on that way," he declared threateningly.

"I should certainly not permit my husband, if I had one, to substitute his conscience for mine." I snapped back.

"It's disgustingly unwomanly," McNair insisted.

I felt that I turned pale. "McNair," I said, in a voice that shook, "I cannot permit you to continue your friendship with an unwomanly woman." With a melodramatic sweep of my hand I indicated that the door was convenient.

McNair rose, a red patch burning in each cheek: "You'll live to rue the day you ordered me out," he prophesized darkly, "and mind, once gone, I'll not come back in a hurry, and you'll be gey lonesome." He stamped out noisily.

And I was lonesome. If I had hated the parade before I hated it doubly now, because it had been the means of separating me from McNair. I cannot tell you why I minded that so much, but the sun seemed not to shine any more with his old brilliance, and the chorus of the birds became discordant chirps; and the great strong free wind, that all spring had lifted my spirit on wings of happiness, became only a wind which blew the dust in my teeth and draped my hair in wisps over my collar; and my business associates were patently fools, and it was queer that I had never before noticed that Winnipeg was such an ugly, dull, windy city.

So the week dragged by.

The day of the parade began with a shower in the early morning, but long before noon the clouds had disappeared, and the wind had dried the streets. Conditions were perfect, and a great crowd turned out to watch.

There is something exhilarating in large numbers of people doing the same thing at the same time, so that in some ways I did not mind the parade as much as I had expected. In others I minded it more. It was rather jolly at the beginning with much laughing and calling back and forth as we got into line and raised our banners, at which the wind tugged hard. But afterward, when we were marching along between the rows of spectators, and listening to the sneering remarks the wind blew to us, and when in the crowd we saw the faces of men we met every day in business and they raised eyebrows of unfeigned surprise, but gave no other sign of recognition, that was very disagreeable.

I tried not to see the spectators, but a horrid fascination drew my eyes to the sidewalk against my will. And there, at a certain busy corner, stood a man and a boy right at the edge of the curb. I caught my breath sharply and steered my eyes straight ahead, but when we came opposite I turned, against my will, against all reason, and stole another glance, and was disconcerted to find McNair staring straight into my face. He gravely lifted his hat and Colin waved at me, but with a cool nod I marched on. Yet because McNair had lifted his hat the day grew brighter, and the wind did not bother me as it had done a little while before.

Presently I was aware that among the boys who were following us was Colin. He sidled over and slipped a piece of paper into my hand and sidled away again.

That paper burned my fingers. It made my palm itch

to open it. I could scarcely wait while we tramped on block after block, up one street and down another, but at last the order was given for dispersal, and I spread out the crumpled note McNair had scribbled on the leaf of a note book. It read:

> You're looking very bonny in your outfit, and I'm proud of you for sticking to the thing you believe to be right, though you're terribly mistaken.
>
> Will you have a bit of dinner with Colin and me to-night? The lad has hardly spoken a civil word to me for a week.
>
> Yours humbly,
>
> McNair.
>
> P.S.—I'll bring along a first-rate wash I have for sore feet.
>
> McN.

There was no sign of Colin or McNair anywhere about, so I went home and washed and dressed and waited. About half-past six two sheepish-looking males came diffidently in the gate, as I saw around the corner of the blind, and marched slowly up the steps, uncertain of their welcome. I had planned that I would be very cold and distant at first, and had settled in my mind just how haughty I would be, but seeing them come shyly up the steps I ran and threw the door wide open and gave each of them a hand and laughed, in order that I might not weep. It was not good policy, as any coquette will tell you, but I loved McNair past all wisdom.

McNair held my hand in his awkwardly, like a lad who

has misbehaved, and would like to have the matter settled on the basis of the least said, soonest mended. When he dropped it he reached down into his pocket and brought out a bottle. "That's that foot wash I mentioned," he said brusquely, and then added in the gentlest tones, "Are you very tired, little woman?"

I had not realised how tired I was until then, but at McNair's tenderness the full consciousness of the fatigue I felt as a result of the long walk after being on my feet all day, rushed in upon me, and I turned and went into my room and sat down in a chair and wept, and wept and wept, a thing I had not done for years.

The two males followed me into the room and shuffled about from one foot to the other, and clucked at me and said "there, there," but I would not be comforted. At last McNair strode over to me, and leaning down, lifted me as if I had been a child and laid me on the couch. "I'll go fetch a doctor," he said, as he propped my head up with a pillow.

I caught his hand, "Don't go," I begged. "All the medicine I need is to have you and Colin back."

He pressed my hand almost fiercely at that; drew his brows together sharply, and his mouth down into deep lines at the corners, and turning his head sideways, stared very hard at the begonia on the bookcase.

"What about supper?" put in the practical Colin.

Mrs. Fleming was entertaining a party of friends, and I would not have her disturbed, but McNair suddenly bethought him of a nearby restaurant and went out to order a meal to be sent in.

As soon as he was gone Colin came over and slipped

his arm about me. "You're awful moist," he commented, "an' you're wetting my sleeve enough to give a fellow the rheumatis."

For answer I sat up and hugged him.

"Aw what are you doing?" he asked, but his voice was not forbidding.

CHAPTER XVIII.
A Discovery.

I find it difficult to write about the 6th of June, 1912. Here and there in our lives a day is burned so deeply into the memory that even time cannot sufficiently soften its outlines to make it a subject for quiet unemotional contemplation.

As I look back upon it now the things that happened that day was not so dreadful, but in those days before the war, when all the cheerful little rills of life trickled leisurely along, it seemed to me to be a catastrophe, and my feeling so made it one.

I remember that day in every little detail. I wakened with a thrill of gladness, as I did every day of that wonderful spring and summer, to the lively marital noises of the sparrows in the maple trees about the house.

Just being alive and in love and seeing the sun streaming in gaily through the window meant happiness. Do people love as blithely, I wonder, in moist, dank climates as we do up in the North, where the hottest day is ushered in by a cool, clear dawn and nearly always fades out into a crisp, chill evening? I doubt it. I know that I found life intoxicating that spring.

And this morning I had an especial occasion for gaiety of spirit. A distinguished party of Old Country journalists was passing through the city, and the local Press folk were making a fête day of it, concluding with a banquet at night to which I was going with McNair. For me to be with McNair always meant happiness in itself.

I smiled contentedly as my eye traveled about the room, resting upon the lacey white things I had laid out to wear, and upon my freshly pressed rose muslin dress, which McNair like better than anything else I had in way of dresses.

I sprang light-heartedly out of bed and ran to the window to take a peep at the sparkling dew-drenched world. It was going to be a perfect day for the automobile ride in the afternoon and the tea at the old fort.

I stopped on my way back for a glance at the new peach-coloured evening gown hanging in my wardrobe, and then I set about cleaning my white shoes, the one thing I had been too tired to attend to the evening before.

While they dried in the sun I dressed and was just slipping my silk-stockinged toes into them, when Mrs. Fleming came in with a box of roses McNair had sent me. It doesn't seem possible that a day with such a propitious beginning could end as miserable as this one did.

I remember thinking as I put on my new white panama with the rose scarf that I was looking particularly well, and why not, since love and happiness have a way of their own of touching the cheeks with rouge and the eyes with fire.

It was planned the Winnipeg people should scatter themselves among the guests so that having a bland, grey-headed Englishman in tow I did not discover until tea-time that McNair was not of the party at old Fort Garry. The realisation brought a slight chill of disappointment, but I reminded myself that he must have been detained unexpectedly at the office, and I concentrated my social energies upon the old gentleman.

The afternoon passed so pleasantly, and we lingered so long that we had to hurry home in the end to dress for the banquet.

I was humming a gay little tune to myself as I pinned a broach into the bosom of my evening dress, when I heard a loud voice asking Mrs. Fleming if I was in. It sounded like McNair and yet unlike.

There came a loud rap at the door and I opened it, and McNair came in. I saw at once that his face was flushed, his eyes bright and staring, and although he was in evening dress he had a dishevelled appearance. "Well, are you ready for the spread, little woman?" he asked, in a high-pitched voice.

I had stopped still, arrested by a sick sort of feeling as I raised my small round arms to fasten the pins more securely in the soft roll of red brown hair at the back of my neck. Perhaps it was my bare arms, from which the sleeves had fallen away to the shoulder, that attracted his attention, but he gave me a quick, surprised look, and advancing he laid a heavy hand on my shoulder and breathed a sickening smell of alcohol into my face.

"You're looking very bonny tonight, my girl," he said gaily. "Will you give me—" He stopped short as I recoiled sick at heart that the first suggestion of intimacy between myself and this man, whom I loved, should come about in this way.

He was not too drunk to understand the hurt expression in my face. He had been bending over me with his lips close to mine, but he straightened up immediately and took his hand from my shoulder.

"I beg your pardon," he said quickly, "I'm not quite myself—some friends from the Old Country in the party."

I was at a loss whether to go to the banquet or stay at home, but in the hope of being some restraint I went. We were a little late, and through some mistake there was only one place left at the head table, which was for McNair, who was going to make a speech. I wanted him to let me sit down quietly at one of the small tables, but he chose rather to make a disturbance about it and refused to sit at the head table at all unless they found a place for me, which occasioned a general shuffle and directed the attention of everyone in the room to us. It was most embarrassing.

I do not remember whether I ate anything at that banquet. I have no recollection of who was on the toast list or what they said. I was so sick with dread of the moment when McNair should be called upon to speak.

It came at last. He rose, and with a hand on the back of my chair began such a funny witty speech that I stared at him incredulously. It was quite a new phase of McNair. I breathed more freely and began to hope it would pass off without any unpleasantness, but towards the end he repeated a story that had brought roars of laughter at the beginning, and I saw the company look at each other significantly, and I know that I blushed to the very tips of my ears. A few more slips made his condition patent to everyone in the room, and when he sat down it was evident that the applause he received was tempered by pity or reprobation, according to the mental attitude of the listener.

To my acute discomfort I was obliged to share in this disagreeable publicity. I know that many of the women gave me a pitying look, supposing that I was his wife. It would serve no purpose to tell in greater detail the events of that evening, of how from gaiety McNair subsided into touchiness, and from that to a dull stupor; of how I was obliged to call a cab myself and take him home when the banquet was over; of how I went on home along with a dead weight at my heart, which a few hours earlier had been so light and gay.

I felt that I had come to an end of my happiness.

*   *   *   *   *

It is one of the tragedies of life—this trek to Canada of men who even in the gentle, humid, unexhilarating climate of the Old Country have developed and unslakable thirst. They come, poor fellows, in the hope of making a new start in the new world. To Canada of all places! To western Canada in particular! Imagine a man who could get up sufficient intensity of thirst to drink to excess in a climate where the end of every avenue is draped in haze; coming for surcease of appetite to these dry, windy plains, where the most distant object meets the brilliant sky with the sharpness of a silhouette; where the night wears no other veil than darkness; and where, even in the hottest July weather the dawn comes tripping over the dewy grass with a tang in her breath. Yet still they come.

Others of their countrymen come also, but of such a phlegmatic type that even the elixir of this buoyant prairie atmosphere cannot stir them to take two glasses where they ought to take only one. There is no possibility of bridging the misunderstanding between this last type of Old Countryman and the Canadian. He has been accustomed to live in a climate where there are families who generation after generation drink in moderation from youth to the grave. He cannot understand, and has no patience with, the social odium the people of Canada try to throw over the practice.

It is difficult to explain to him that in every country there is a principle of self-preservation which moves society to discountenance those customs which are a peculiar menace to its existence: that morality is chiefly a matter of humidity and altitude.

It is to this instinct of self-preservation rather than to any high ethical qualities that I attribute the attitude of the people of Canada towards the consumption of alcohol. I do not refer merely to its prohibition, but to the social stigma that as long as I can remember has fallen upon men who were known to be habitual drinkers. In Canada in a very large percentage of cases drinking means drunkenness and drunkenness means the same thing everywhere—poverty. Therefore in the circle of society in which I was raised men who drank were regarded as ineligible. Many charming young girls married them, but their friends looked on with fear and trembling, and saw the wash-tub as a means of livelihood threatening them in the distance. Sometimes their fears were realised, sometimes not, but the fear was so general and so deep-seated that I think the number who escaped misery of a greater or lesser degree must have been small.

This explanation has been offered here to try to make

clear the attitude of the average Canadian woman, herself a total abstainer, towards the man who drinks. It should be added that I cannot speak for the women of the brothels or of the top layer of society, both of whom I have heard often indulge quite freely, but not having the acquaintance of either I am not in a position to give authentic information.

Myself, I belong to the bourgeoisie, "that almost people," as Victor Hugo calls us, and which at that is a liberal compliment compared with Mr. Bernard Shaw's ardent dispraise of us.

If we had a peasant class in Canada I should elect to belong to that, but we have not. Contradictory as it may sound we have only two classes of society here: a middle class or bourgeoisie and an aristocracy of wealth.

It is true that some of our rich people have acquired titles, so many, in fact, and frequently for such peculiar services to their country that it has begun to seem to the people of Canada, that is, to the confirmed bourgeoisie, that the British Government would do well to follow the example of the diamond merchants. Geologists have said that there are enough diamonds in the world to make diamonds as cheap as imitation pearls, but the merchants keep them off the market and put a high price on those that are for sale.

Recently a Canadian newspaper said of a certain public man who had done his utmost to corrupt the civic life of his country, that he would soon be sufficiently disqualified as a citizen to receive a title. The statement was an exaggeration, for many admirable Canadians have, very regrettably it seems to me, accepted this left-over badge of an out-grown feudal system. But it is a healthy sign that Canada laughed.

* * * * *

Without the foregoing explanation of the attitude of the great middle class of society of Canada towards the drinking of intoxicating liquor it would be impossible to make anybody outside of the Dominion comprehend the misery I experienced the night of the banquet.

Even so a person brought up with another background would doubtless think my grief at finding McNair a drinking man disproportionate to the offence, for I knew that whether or not he drank, McNair was the cleanest minded, sweetest-natured man I had ever met. Nevertheless I wept my heart out that night.

For weeks and weeks I had been thinking of marrying McNair and had looked with indulgent eyes upon his little faults, intending to break him gently of them later on. And I had planned pretty surprises for his home-comings that would make those dear dark eyes of his lighten up with a pleased tenderness.

Then one day my castle of dreams had fallen to ruins. Not because McNair had been drunk once, but because there rushed back into my mind little things he and Colin had said which made it clear that he had been fighting this thing for years and had never mastered it. I had not understood them at the time, but their purport now became obvious.

Ahead loomed poverty and sordidness, perhaps quarrelling and recrimination, from which my mind shrank away in distaste. Under the most propitious circumstances enough bloom is brushed from the romance by matters of laundry, Easter hats, boiled eggs and household accounts. Add to this poverty and uncertainty, and what chance was there that the beautiful thing between McNair and myself would survive? It seemed to me that our love was like a ball of crystal reflecting our dazzling northern skies. I could not endure that it should be clouded by mean, ugly, humiliating poverty and shame.

I wanted so much that I would be ashamed to set it down here for fear of being thought unwomanly, that McNair should take me in his big arms and press his lips against mine, but I wanted, too, that his eyes should keep that look of deep manly tenderness with which he looked at me when he took my little hand and held it so long and caressingly in his big one.

Perhaps that was too much to ask of life. At any rate I felt that I had been denied it. I could see no way out as I lay there in the dark and tried vainly to slip from under the weight of this horrid reality.

CHAPTER XIX.
A Poor Fighter.

It was more than a week before I saw McNair again. Sitting one evening on the bench near the fence, where I was protected from the inquisitive eyes of the passer-by by the high Caragana hedge, I glanced up from my book and saw him standing just inside the gate. It hurt me to see the look of shame and diffidence in his eyes, so I rose quickly and held out both hands to him.

I felt his large hands tremble as he folded them about my little ones. He didn't speak, but after what seemed a long time a tear splashed on my wrist. He dropped my hands abruptly, strode away and stood beside the maple tree. Resting his elbow on a branch and his head on his hand he stared into the slowly deepening twilight.

I sat down on the bench again and waited. Presently I heard his heavy step and the bench creaked beneath his weight, but I did not look up until he reached over and laid his hand on mine.

"Why didn't you upbraid me?" he said, huskily.

"Because I know how hard you've been trying," I answered, looking up pityingly into his troubled grey eyes.

His fingers closed convulsively over mine.

"How do you understand so well?" he murmured. "You who go as straight as an arrow to the goal. I thought you would have no patience with weakness. I was even afraid to come back to you—but I was so lonely—" he broke off abruptly and looked at me appealingly, his face drawn down into deep haggard lines.

"It's because I'm a poor fighter myself," I replied. "Yes, I am," I insisted, waving aside his indignant protest. "You don't see the shrinking spirit I drag after me into every conflict. You don't see how uncomfortable I am before the spoken derision of people for whose minds and ideals of like I have no respect. My intelligence rises above it, but there is some thing in me, a servility whipped into me in my childhood, that makes me almost ashamed of the truth as I see it."

"But you go on fighting?"

"Doggedly, not bravely," I confessed. "You had no idea, I suppose, that the reason I was so angry with you about that suffrage parade was that I wanted to do what you advised and leave that which I knew ought to be done to someone else."

McNair looked at me in amazement. "I see," he said after awhile, and he got up from the bench and began to walk up and down with his hands clasped behind his back. Finally he stopped in front of me.

"Did you ever read Martin Chuzzelwit?" he said abruptly.

I nodded.

"Then, my dear girl, I submit you are like Mark Tapley," he went on. "When the occasion arises you will 'come out strong,' and when that time comes I give you my word that I shall not stand between you and the thing you believe to be right."

Neither of us suspected the strange dark days that were ahead, nor could we have guessed how McNair would keep this lightly given promise.

CHAPTER XX.
Pauline Intervenes.

There had been a big July hailstorm some fifty miles away, and all the day following Winnipegers went about with chattering teeth. The bright midsummer sun did its best, but the cold wind swept in upon us from the hailed region and drove us into doorways while we waited for street cars, and sent us slinking along in the shelter of high buildings.

Pauline having announced her intention of coming to spend the evening with me, I had prepared an open fire, to which she drew up gratefully. She dropped into McNair's chair, stretched her long limbs out, and clasped her hands behind her head.

"You room smells suspiciously of tobacco smoke, Aleta," she said, turning her head sideways to look at me.

McNair had called in a few minutes before on his way to the office to bring me a book, but that was no affair of Pauline's.

"Maybe I've taken to the weed," I answered evasively. I suspected she had come to advise me about McNair.

"Smells like a certain Scotsman's pipe," she persisted.

I blushed, but said nothing, while I looked very straight at the fire.

"Aleta," I could feel that her eyes were resting upon me disapprovingly, "I think you had better be careful, dear," she said gently, "He is a very charming man, and you might learn to care more for him than was good for your peace of mind."

Just as if our affections were open to advice! But Pauline is like that. She will fall in love with a judge or the head of a great corporation, and he will be a man of exemplary habits and a pillar of the church, not that the two necessarily go together, but they will in Pauline's husband.

I looked at her as she leaned back in the chair; at her tailored skirt, made by a man, whose label the vain wearer finds ways of displaying to envious feminine eyes, and at her smartly tailored blouse, and I thought how efficient she was. She would never have been foolish enough to fall in love with a man at first sight, without knowing anything about him, and whether he was a proper person to be loved.

As I continued silent, Pauline resumed her role of Providence deciding my destiny for me.

"That night at the banquet—"

"Pauline," I interrupted her quietly, "you have no occasion to worry about McNair and me; but, if you please, we will not discuss his faults."

I think I must have spoken with some firmness, for Pauline subsided immediately. She removed a bone pin from her dark roll of hair to cover a certain embarrassment.

To atone for my seeming rudeness to a guest I asked hastily: "How is your washerwoman getting along, Pauline?"

"It's a very sad case," she replied, and she related with much feeling the story of Mrs. Jackson's woes.

"Your stories amaze me," I said, when she had finished. "Every case of poverty, except that with which you come personally in contact is due to stubbornness on the part of the poor, and you will fight to the last ditch against any measures that are proposed to eliminate the causes of misery, and yet you get all worked up about the fruits of the system you are upholding whenever it invades you backyard."

"And you Radicals amaze me," Pauline aptly retorted. "You make a deafening row about the poor, and yet when you come across a case like that of Mrs. Jackson you just make a fresh onslaught on the system and leave her and her bairns to starve. To parody Mr. Dooley, 'God help the poor when they fall into the hands of their friends.'"

I laughed and got up and sat on the arm of Pauline's chair, and slipped my arm about her neck and kissed her.

Pauline smiled.

"Very likely the world needs all different types of human being or we wouldn't be here," I said, and we began to gossip about local affairs and forgot our differences.

CHAPTER XXI.
The Church.

"Would you like to come to church with me this morning?" McNair asked, appearing unexpectedly before me, where I sat on the garden seat in the pleasant quiet of a sunny Sabbath morning.

He was dressed in a new brown suit of tweeds, and was looking so fine that it was difficult to refuse him anything; nevertheless I answered firmly, "Indeed I will not."

McNair reached down into the pockets of his coat, brought out his pipe, struck a match on the sole of his tan shoe, lit the pipe and puffed awhile in silence.

I moved over and he sat down, creakingly, on the end of the bench. He took his pipe out of his mouth, blew the smoke up towards the bright blue sky, turned and laid his long arm along the back of the seat, and looked at me gravely.

"We haven't spoken much about religion. You're not an atheist, are you?" he asked, anxiously.

He looked relieved when I answered, "Not even an Agnostic."

"There was a time," I went on, "when I had disposed of the soul, but I began to study history and my faith in a spiritual world came back to me."

McNair looked interested. "How is that?" he inquired.

"I found that all down the centuries the world has produced great men and women who have had a light within;

people who have said to their persecutors, and they were always persecuted, 'Do with this physical body of mine what you will; I see life the way I have said and I will not lie about it to please you.'

"The fact that a few great beings have lived who have defied their own bodies and the whole physical world by which they were surrounded would, I think, be strong evidence of a soul, but we have the added fact that the tortures to which they are subjected by a baffled and enraged physical world, instead of driving men away from their ideas, draws the spiritually minded to them. So I have come to believe again that there is probably a soul, and if a soul, why not a God?"

"Then what is your objection to the Church?" McNair asked in surprise.

"The fact that the Church has been one of the most ardent persecutors of these supremely great souls who have dared to follow the light. Founded by a rebel and an outcast from society, a despised soap-box orator, it has become the leading hound in the pack of social tyrannies with which to try to drive the fine free souls of men to uniformity of thought."

"Do you know what I think of God?" I continued, explosively, for McNair had happened to touch a point where I felt very intensely.

He shook his head helplessly.

"I think God is a democrat, the only democrat, in fact. He has filled the world with human beings no two of whom are alike, and I think, indeed, I am sure, he meant them to be left free to develop their differences and to report of life as they saw it, and He knew that human nature was so good and clean at heart that only the beautiful would survive.

"But, unfortunately, there have arisen certain madmen who think themselves gods; men who say by their conduct 'I am made on a special last, different from the rest of my fellowmen. Therefore, I will set myself up as a judge of the drawings other men make of life, and I will rub out those that displease me lest others not so wise and godlike as myself might see them and come to harm thereby.'

"So they have gone ruthlessly about in the world of art, science, literature and politics, wiping out the lovely things that grow out of unusual minds. They may have erased a few ugly pictures, which would have faded of themselves, for it is a proven fact that no merely obscene play or book ever lives, but they have done their utmost to destroy the warmth, fragrance and beauty of life."

"But about the Church?" McNair put in mildly, in an attempt to bring me back to the original issue.

"Well," I said, more quietly, "many of these self-elected supermen have operated in and through the Church, and the Church, as an institution, has promoted their activities. It is an interesting fact that the Church which has made the greatest contribution to human freedom is the one which is conducted democratically with no preachers to act as middlemen between folk and their God."

McNair sat thoughtful for some time; puff, puff, puffing away at his pipe.

"I think you're not very consistent," he said at last. "When I have pointed out to you the faults of some of the advocates of your suffrage cause, you have answered that an organisation must not be condemned because some of the people who belong to it are prone to err. Doesn't that apply to the Church also?"

"I don't think so," I answered, "because with the Church it's the other way about. Both in the clergy and the laity there have been magnificent individuals, but as an institution it has been almost unfailingly on the side of despotism and persecution. The Church has not seen, any more than the avowed materialists, that an idea cannot be conquered by prisons or death sentences, but only with another idea bigger and finer than itself. That is the one great outstanding fact written in letters of blood and fire across the page of history, but the world seems to be blind."

We fell into a thoughtful silence, which I broke by rising and saying coaxingly: "In the meantime, McNair, while the world is waiting for us to point out these tremendous truths in it, let us go out to the prairie and pick orange lilies."

"Run along and get your bonnet then," he said, smiling at me indulgently.

We walked along for sometime in silence. Presently I laid my hand lightly on his arm: "Sometimes I've wondered if our friendship was not a mistake," I said timidly. "We look at life so differently."

McNair seemed not to hear. He merely took his pipe from his mouth and pointed the amber stem at the horizon, where great soft white cloud domes were piling themselves one upon another.

"There'll be rain before night," he remarked.

But later, when we were out on the open prairie and I had gathered my arm full of orange lilies, he laid his hand on my shoulder, "Promise me," he said, and there was a queer look in his eyes, "that you will never say that again."

"Say what?" I asked in surprise.

"That our friendship is a mistake. To me, at least, it is the most precious experience this niggardly old world has given me."

I was at a loss for a reply, but was saved the necessity of making one, for he looked down at my feet and said indignantly, "Woman, you are trampling on a lily."

CHAPTER XXII.
The Broken Spell.

It would be pleasant if I could relate that my friendship immediately saved McNair from his weakness, but it did not. After that first outbreak he did not touch a drop for five weeks, and then came a week when he did not draw a sober breath, and when Colin and I were most unhappy.

He was very haughty and defiant of my disapproval when the passion for liquor was upon him; and deeply penitent and touchingly grateful for my continued friendship when it was over. Indeed, that was pretty well the history of the two years that followed.

"I don't deserve you friendship, little woman," he said, one day when he dropped into my office, "but I need it. Take away from a man the one chance more to make good—and then what?"

"Never mind the answer, McNair," I replied, "as long as we both live I shall be your friend, and I'll argue with you and argue with you to your heart's content."

"If the flimsy ground you have for your outlandish opinions can be called argument," he retorted, grinning at me.

"Let's see what you have in your page this week," he said, taking the proof from under my hand.

I watched his glance travel over the sheet. All at once he stopped, and began to read carefully. His breath came in short pants of indignation. His face grew crimson and his eyes glaring.

"Rot….damnable….liar," he exploded at intervals.

Finally he crushed the proof into a ball and threw it to the far side of the room.

"Is the woman who wrote that letter within walking distance?" he inquired hoarsely.

"The author was a member of your own fair sex, sir."

"The scoundrel! If ever I lay my hands on him I'll thrash him within an inch of his life."

"And you'll not prove him wrong by that method," I replied.

"But why print such a crude, insulting thing? Couldn't you get anything else to fill up your space?"

"Nothing," I answered, "that would be such good propaganda for the suffrage cause."

"I don't see that," McNair growled. "What has this virulent attack on you to do with it?"

"Breeds confidence, and gives people a sense of security. I have always thought there was no greater flash of genius in the Bible than that sentence: 'And ye shall know the truth, and the truth shall make you free.'"

"That's a beautiful theory," McNair retorted, "but this fellow has abused his freedom."

"And greatly helped our cause thereby."

"Mind you this, McNair," I said, shaking my finger under his nose, "there is no cause but a bad one which thrives on the suppression of argument."

McNair caught my hand in his and held it firmly, and he looked long and tenderly into my eyes, so that I forgot about feminism and democracy, and remembered only that my hand lay in the clasp of the man I loved.

A flood of colour surged over my face and neck, and I trembled like a leaf.

At that a great light leaped in McNair's eyes, and he leaned toward me so that I could feel his breath warm on my cheek.

There came a loud rap at the door.

"What is it?" I asked sharply.

"Telephone," sang out the girl on the other side of the partition as casually as if she had not interrupted one of the great moments of a person's life.

The spell was broken.

To this day the sight of that girl's bleached hair and alabaster nose is distasteful to me.

CHAPTER XXIII.
McNair's Story.

My first shock of disappointment at finding McNair a drinking man subsided and I began to persuade myself that if I married him he would give it up for my sake and for the sake of the children with which I hoped our union would be blessed. I was very anxious to believe that, I refused to think of the many cases I had known of the women who had married men to reform them and failed. I could think of only two who had succeeded. Everything I could find about building up the health to resist the drink habit I read, and began to hope that if I gave an intelligent scientific study to the question great things might be accomplished.

Even when McNair came to me one evening red-eyed, flushed and half-dazed with the headache I was not daunted. I made him lie down on the couch and brought a big basin of ice water and bathed his head until the fiery heat had subsided.

"That will do, thank you," he said at last, "my head is much better."

I crossed over to the tea table and brought a cup of strong coffee I had brewing.

His hand shook so as he held it out that I drew the cup away and raised it with my own hand to his lips.

He drank the coffee down quickly, wiped his lips and

touched my hand with them. "It's a very precious little hand," he said, smiling.

I did not reply and he looked at me quickly, so quickly that he caught the expression the touch of his lips on my hand had brought to my face.

We were both embarrassed. His face grew grave, and he sat shading his eyes with his hand. At last he sat up straight and took a long breath.

"Tell me, little woman," he asked anxiously, "would you ever forgive a person who had deceived you about something very important?"

"That would depend upon what it was," I answered, with a miserable foreboding of disaster.

"Supposing it was—"

"Oh, please tell me what it is," I broke in, unable to bear the suspense any longer.

His hand shook as he moved it uneasily up and down the lapel of his coat. "Very well," he blurted out, "I had no right to take your friendship without telling you that I am not placed like other men that—that—in fact, I am a married man."

I rose hastily and walked away, hoping to conceal the blow this was to me. Feeling dizzy I stopped with my arm resting on the bookcase to steady myself. I have no idea how long I stood there, but I was conscious of McNair coming to me and taking my hand and leading me to a chair.

He began speaking to me in a quiet, gentle voice. "I want to tell you the whole story, if you will listen to me. Many times I have wanted to tell you, but there is something you won't understand, and it is that one may have been so hurt by some experience of one's life that to speak of it is like putting a knife into an open sore.

"I think I told you I was turned out on the world alone at fourteen when my mother died. Before that, with having to add enough to her little pension to keep us living, and take care of her at nights, and learn the lessons she set me I had no time to run the streets and learn the things some boys do about life. After she went I did as she asked me to, worked in the day time and went to night school, so that I lived quite apart from other young people in a dream world of my own, with the memory of my mother as the one beautiful thing upon which I looked back.

"I worked in a tailor shop in the day-time and went to night school until I was between seventeen and eighteen, when I took a clerical position at which I hoped to make enough to put myself through college. Then one night I went to a cheap variety show and there I saw the girl and became infatuated with her. She was a singer and dancer, and I thought her the most beautiful creature I had ever seen in my life. In my inexperience I assumed that she was as good as she was beautiful." McNair shuddered suggestively.

"Well, to make a long story short I was married to her a week later." He covered his face with his hands. "She was a terrible woman," he went on at last, taking his hands away, and turning a grey face towards me. "She was unclean as you cannot conceive of the meaning of that word. She—she was—" He broke off and began to walk up and down with his hands clenched until the tips of his fingers were white. "I cannot tell you what she was," he continued, "but after two months I came home one night to find that she had taken everything of value in the place and gone off with another man, and left a coarse, insulting note informing me of the fact."

"But if it was as long ago as that you must be free by now," I suggested diffidently.

He shook his head. "Only if you have reason to believe them dead. She has looked me up every few years and begged from me, and it was so hateful to see her that I gave her something to go away.

"I wonder if you can understand how sensitive I have always been about this. I took to drink to try to forget it, but it is not a very sure cure for brooding. I think I would have foundered altogether had it not been for Colin's father whom I had met a short time before, and who, being older, and knowing the circumstances, took me in hand and made me brace up. Then he left me Colin, and finally I came out here and found you. Maybe you won't understand the temptation it was to have the friendship of a good woman after what I had been through and my years of loneliness … but I didn't mean to be cruel to you … I have never thought of myself as married … though, to be honest, I guess I would have yielded to the temptation of your friendship, as I have yielded to other temptations, no matter how much married I had been …. for I needed you so badly, and wanted so terribly the thing you have brought into my life." He fell silent, and I sat turning what he had told me over in my mind without speaking.

Presently he touched my hand diffidently. "What are you going to do about it?" he asked anxiously.

"Nothing," I answered, roused from my reverie, "unless spoil you more than ever, to make up for those barren years. What did you suppose I'd do?"

McNair sat blinking at me in amazement. "You are the most astounding woman," he exclaimed. "In big things like this, where I expect you to go up in the air, you are so quiet and reasonable, and then again you'll threaten to break off our friendship over some silly thing, like the other night when I said I didn't see anything the matter with McDonald telling his wife not to go to a certain show."

"It's your sense of proportion that's wrong, McNair. Your having made a mistaken marriage when you were a boy is not a serious matter and can be repaired, but for one person to act as the proprietor of another is a crime. It is a local expression of all the intolerable tyranny in the world."

McNair threw up his hands. "All right, I agree, only don't give me a lecture on feminism to-night, for I am not in proper fighting trim. I'm prepared to surrender to you unconditionally. You stand by a fellow so in tight places. I—I never knew women were like that. Even my mother would fall down on big things sometimes."

I laid my little hand on his arm. "Why didn't you tell me months ago. You would have been so much happier if you had."

He took my hand in his. "I'm having some detectives in the Old Country try to find her," he said, ignoring my spoken question and answering my thoughts, "and I hope to get clear of the thing before long. In the meantime if you'll give me the benefit of your friendship, as you have in the past, I'll be grateful."

We left it at that, afraid of ourselves, perhaps, if we broke down the barrier of reserve between us, and hoping that our lips would soon be unsealed. But two years crept away and the Old Country detectives whom McNair had employed, found no trace of the woman.

In the small personal city in which we lived, and with our up-bringing, any other than a legal union was impossible. Sometimes I thought of it, but I never hinted it to McNair nor he to me.

CHAPTER XXIV.
War.

Then the war came. It burst like a cloud upon our holidaying world, and set us all a-tremble and a-thrill.

Germany had broken the peace of the world and plunged us into night. Very well, we would collect a few Canadians and send them over and they would settle the matter in a few months and come home, and we would give them a banquet, and allow them to die in the poorhouse, as had been done to the heroes of other wars.

What days those were! An extra every half-hour! War maps in every hand! A half mile towards Paris—gloom for two days! A great ship sunk—gloom for a week! Our hearts were sensitive to suffering then and the death of a hundred thousand men meant something to us. The blood reeked in our nostrils.

Yet for all that we women, old men and cripples, how we did shout our patriotism from the housetops, so that nobody should miss our voice in the great songs.

What days those were!

The even tramp of troops along the streets! The morning call of the bugle! The thrill of an hourly excitement! The awful torment of soul as one read of rivers full of dead bodies. Human bodies! It broke our hearts to read of men with their legs and arms blown off; with their faces shattered to pieces; men who would go on living under the most horrible physical limitations. That was early in the war before we had grown callous to the pain of other human beings.

And yet, mixed with our horror, there was a thrill, a feeling that something had really happened in our time.

What days those were!

CHAPTER XXV.
Then It Came Home.

One evening in October, McNair, whose recent conduct had been discouraging, came to see me. We talked about many things, and when the evening was well advanced, and I was making him a cup of chocolate, he announced, in the droll spectacular way men have, "I've enlisted," just as casually as if he had not been thinking of it the whole evening.

I was dumbfounded. "McNair!" was all I could find breath to say, as I paused with the sugar tongs poised in the air.

McNair looked modestly heroic, and I felt—I cannot tell you how I felt. Glad that he was not afraid to face physical danger; afraid of that danger for him; sick at heart at the thought that we were to be parted; appalled at the possibility that the parting might be for ever.

McNair was full of the new life and had high hopes that in the change he would find the remedy for his besetting weakness. I had my doubts of war as a reformatory, but I kept them to myself. There are times when the doubter is intolerable, and I knew that this was one of them.

Moreover, I had a very strange conviction about McNair, that some day he would square away. The coming of this conviction was the only thing approaching a psychic experience I ever had in my life.

I was sitting in my room one night worrying about McNair, when all at once it seemed as if someone had said, "Don't worry; he is going to give it up." Immediately I had a sense of the most utter peace. The impression was so vivid that I wrote a note to him at once and told him of it.

He was very deeply touched. I suppose I wrote very convincingly under the impulse of that spiritual uplift, for I received a very beautiful letter in reply.

I don't think he gave a thought to the supernatural suggestion, but he was intensely appreciative of my faith in him and my concern for his welfare.

After that I went about looking resentfully at all the able-bodied men I met, whom I felt had as much right to go as McNair. That is the first of the many internal hates war breeds; the first of a whole army of ugly, primitive, degrading emotions, which tend to drag humanity back to barbarism. It seemed to me too, that babies sprang up like toadstools in the homes of young married couples, and that with each new baby the young man added a louder and fresher note to the chorus of patriotism.

The suspicion that these little folks were a war risk insurance may have grown out of the ill-thinking of my own mind, and the idea that the young man grew more noisy as his personal safety increased may have been the fruit of a diseased imagination. I know that there is no more unprofitable occupation than assigning motives for other people's conduct. Each one of us has one great task sufficient to absorb all our energies if we performed it creditably, which is to bring the average of our conduct up so that our own best moments may not be used against us as an evidence of hypocrisy.

But my heart was very sore at the thought of losing the dear man about whom the dreams of my life centred, and my anxiety bred in me a hysteria of fear and hate.

To relieve my mind I plunged into Red Cross work, and one Saturday afternoon at one of the sewing circles, a woman, whom I had always regarded as a very mild and reasonable person, said in answer to a lament about the air raids, "Those German swine will all have to be killed off." In and out went the needles.

"Yes, indeed," sighed the fat little lady near the door, who sat with her toes braced against the floor, because she was too short for her chair and had need of a lap, "indeed they will. They killed me nevvy last week. It's just awful the things they do."

"And the lies they tell," put in Pauline, "you can't believe a word of their reports."

A little silver-haired old lady threaded her needle, and then, sticking it in the bosom of her dress, looked up at Pauline. "I've thought sometimes, my dear," she said mildly, "that our own reports are a little biased. I noticed this morning that we had re-taken a town that the reports had not mentioned was lost."

An awful silence fell upon the room; a silence full of electricity.

When I looked up Pauline had fixed the silver-haired lady with a glaring eye. "Do you mean to insinuate, Mrs. Mayhew, that the British government would say anything that isn't true?"

The silver-haired lady blushed, under the cold regard of the meeting, and retracted the insinuation without reservation or equivocation.

"As I was saying," resumed the first speaker, "the Germans have got to be crushed." Everybody agreed that they had.

It was in the early days of the war before the editorial writers, those dauntless heroes of the swivel chair, had transferred the crushing from the German nation to German militarism.

CHAPTER XXVI.
Ned in Difficulties.

During the two years and more that I had become intimate with McNair I had seen very little of Ned Grant, so that I was rather surprised to get a telephone message from him one evening asking me if he might come over to see me. When he came he was very quiet and abstracted, and I knew that he had something on his mind.

He had been sitting for some time in his customary position of thought, with his hands clasped between his knees, when he looked up at me abruptly and said, "I guess we don't grow up much, Aleta?"

"Who doesn't?" I asked, in surprise.

"We men," he explained, smiling. "Whenever we stub our toes or burn our fingers we run for all we're worth to some woman, on whose sympathy we can rely, for a little petting."

"What particular form do the burnt fingers take this time?" I questioned, touched, as I think a woman always is, by that dependence of a man on her tenderness.

He looked embarrassed. "I can't explain very well—couldn't you pet a fellow in a general way, perhaps, without knowing all the particulars?"

I shook my head in the negative. "No sir, I won't prescribe without knowing the symptoms."

"Maybe you won't do it then, but it's this," he explained. "I was put out of a club to-day to which I have belonged for years, because of my opposition to the war."

I caught my breath sharply. "That was a real burn, wasn't it Ned?"

"It is the most unpleasant experience I have ever had in my life. I resigned, but they wouldn't accept my resignation in order to have the pleasure of expelling me."

"Oh, how mean!" I exclaimed, indignantly.

"What do you think of the war, anyway, Aleta?" He asked.

I got up and put some more coal on the fire. "I have been trying very hard not to think," I said, as I resumed my seat. "I'd like so much to go with the majority in this one thing—especially—" I broke off, unable to speak of McNair to Ned.

He saw my meaning at once. "Of course, it would be better for you—" His voice trailed off into a sigh.

The conservative pictures the man who opposes authority as a jaunty seeker after the limelight of publicity, who enjoys being expelled from clubs and cut dead by old friends on the street. It is a comfortable way to think of him, for it makes his persecution a so much pleasanter matter. The radical at a distance of either a locality or time is apt to imagine him a great commanding hero. Often, as a matter of fact, he is a drab medium-sized man like Ned, discouraged and saddened by his social isolation, but going doggedly on, impelled by some unknown law to follow the stony path of resistance.

To-night he was the very personification of loneliness and dejection, and my heart was deeply stirred. I leaned towards him suddenly. "Listen, Ned," I said, "even suppose I am not very clear on this thing, that is no reason why I should not stand by you and keep you from getting too blue, is it?"

Ned's face brightened, then darkened. "There would be considerable social odium involved in being known to be my friend," he suggested, hesitatingly.

"I don't mind that," I lied, with all the fluency at my command. There has never been a time when I did not mind social odium, but one cannot be altogether a cad. So I made Ned promise to look me up whenever the way became too hard.

CHAPTER XXVII.
Colin in a Fury.

One afternoon Colin came dashing into my office, slammed the door after him, threw his cap on my typewriter table, and stood glaring at me, his eyes blazing and his hair standing out every way.

"McNair's a fool," he shouted, furiously.

I nodded and motioned him to a chair, which he did not take. He stood awkwardly before me, his lips working and his fist clenching and unclenching.

"And I'm going to leave him," he exploded further.

I moved the chair toward him with the toe of my shoe. "Tell me about it, Colin," I encouraged him.

He dropped on to the chair and sat there tense, with a hand on each knee, and leaned toward me belligerently.

"Well?" I asked.

He licked his lips, blushed, and began. "Well, it was like this, McNair overtook Jenny Daly and me coming home from a picture show last night, and what does he do but come along with us and begin to talk smart."

"Talk smart," I repeated.

"Yes; silly stuff about I'd got old enough to kiss girls, and first thing he knew I'd be wanting to get married. You know."

I knew Colin was keeping something back, so I looked him straight in the eye and said "And?"

Colin shuffled his feet. "There's half-a-dozen of us young folks that go to the show together, and Jenny told the others I'd been blabbing—and—they dropped me to-day—and it's all McNair's fault."

I thought it over a little. "Colin," I said at last, "McNair did act unwisely, but he can't get it into his head that you're a man. He thinks you are still a little boy."

The word man went a long way to appease Colin's wrath.

"It's time he did then," he said, still indignantly, but with subsiding rage. "It isn't as if he hadn't kissed plenty of girls himself."

I was thunderstruck. "What's that you say, Colin?" I asked, quickly.

Colin, who had picked up his cap again, twirled it in his hands. "Well, I saw him once, in Edinburgh, when he was half seas over, kiss the chambermaid in the hotel where we were staying, and likely he has kissed plenty more."

I gave a relieved laugh; I was not much afraid of the competition of chambermaids.

I drew my chair close up to Colin's and we had a long talk about things which shall not be set down here, since they are nobody's business but our own.

When we parted at the door Colin said: "It's a good thing for McNair that he had the sense to take up with a woman like you."

And I answered: "Be sure and tell him I want to see him to-night."

I put a fire in the grate that evening, partly because a grate fire always puts McNair in good humour, partly because it is an excellent first aid to difficult conversations.

As it transpired it was not needed for amiability, for McNair was in one of his rare fits of gaiety that evening.

"The little lad told me the woman wanted to see me," he said, smiling, as he divested himself of his overcoat and laid a box of chocolates on the table.

That was the first intimation I had of the fact, confirmed later by Colin, that these two men folk always called me "The Woman" between them.

"What little lad," I asked, after he had stretched himself to his full length in his special easy chair and filled his pipe.

He took the pipe from his mouth; watched a white curl of smoke ascend toward the ceiling. "Colin, of course," he replied, quite casually, when the last ring of vapour had disappeared.

I leaned back in my low rocker and clasped my hands behind my head. "Did it never strike you, McNair," I asked, "that Colin isn't a little lad any longer?"

McNair turned to me with a laugh. "I've a good joke to tell you about that. I caught the little beggar going home with a girl last night."

"Yes, and talked so foolishly that Colin came to me to-day threatening to leave you."

"W-h-a-t?"

Then I told him the whole story, both what Colin had told me and what he had implied.

"So he had kissed the little sliver," he laughed, when I had finished.

"Scores of time, no doubt, and they thought he had been tattling and dropped him."

McNair chuckled. "The little beggar's beginning young

enough. Good thing they dropped him though."

"McNair," I said, looking hard at the fire, "I want to say something to you."

"Say on," McNair replied, in a light tone that made my task more difficult.

"I think you ought to have a talk with Colin," I said.

"What about?" he inquired, casually.

"About all those things which a father would rather tell his son that have him find them out from other boys," I answered.

McNair gave me a quick surprised look as he rose and laid his pipe on the table.

"You're all the father he has," I added, as he began tramping up and down the room, with his hands clasped behind his back.

On one of his rounds of the room he stopped behind my chair, and, laying his hand on my head, he turned my face back so that he could look down into my eyes.

"The boy needs a mother," he said, with a meaning smile.

"Which boy?" I asked, impertinently.

It was an unhappy speech, for his face clouded. "Both of us," he answered. "If only it were possible." And he turned away and commenced his walk again.

Later I felt a very light touch on my head once more, and I might have thought that also was his hand if the mirror above my little mantel had not registered the truth more accurately than my sense of touch.

CHAPTER XXVIII.
Farewell.

McNair was sitting in the big chair, smoking in silence, as he had sat ever since he came in.

"Are you quite well?" I asked at last.

He started. "Certainly; why?" he inquired, in surprise.

"You've been here twenty minutes by the clock, and you haven't started an argument yet."

He turned to me with a smile. "We're not going to argue to-night, little woman," he said, with a peculiar inflection in his voice. "This may be our last night together for some time."

I gripped the arm of my chair and bit my lip till it bled.

"I am going to camp to-morrow," he went on. "I might get leave to come back for a week-end, but in case I don't there are some things we must talk over."

Still I could not speak.

He leaned over and took my hand, and we sat thus in silence, while the ebony clock on the mantel ticked away our precious minutes.

"I'm going to leave you Colin," he said at last. "He'll be our boy for the period of the war—and perhaps—if I come back—I'll be a free man and a decent one—" He broke off completely, dropped my hand, rose, and began to walk up and down the room, gnawing his short military mustache fiercely.

That "if" made me sick at heart, but I looked at McNair as bravely as I could, and said: "McNair, you will come back, and sometime it will be all right—and—and we—" I found it impossible to finish the sentence.

McNair stopped and looked down at me. "Will nothing shake your faith in me?" he asked. "After these last months and the way I've neglected you for weeks at a time."

"I believe I'm incurable," I answered.

McNair laid his hand on the back of my chair and stood smiling at me. "A man ought to be able to put up a good fight with such a cause and such backing."

A shadow fell upon my spirit, and I turned my head away.

At that he came around, moved his chair up close to mine and sat down. Then he leaned over and gently drew away the hand I had placed over my eyes and held it firmly in his own.

"I want you to tell me what's worrying you, little woman," he demanded, quietly.

"I cannot," I replied, resolutely.

"Then you're not playing fair with me," he declared, frowning. "For nearly three years I have unloaded every care of mine on to your shoulders."

I caught my breath sharply. It was so precious to feel such protecting tenderness at hand. Still I resisted it. "This is the one thing," I said, "that I really cannot tell you or I would."

"Then I know," he said. "It's that you don't believe in the righteousness of the war."

I was amazed at his insight. "How did you guess?" I stammered, taken aback.

"Do you remember that Sunday when I wanted you to go to church and you wouldn't?"

I nodded.

McNair went on: "You made it quite clear to me that day that your mind would nearly always register opposition to the accepted thing, not because you wanted it to but because you are constituted that way. When the war came I expected you to fall out with it before long."

I looked at McNair in astonishment too great for words.

"I wanted to know," he concluded, "whether it had happened yet."

"Why?" I asked, quickly.

"Because I wanted to tell you while we were together that nothing like that need ever come between us."

I laid my head against McNair's sleeve and sprinkled tear-drops upon it.

I felt his muscles tighten up. I knew that my head against his arm was a great temptation, and to-night I wanted it to be so. I had thrown discretion to the winds. With two words McNair could have picked me up and carried me off to be his wife in fact, at least.

But this night McNair was strong. Tenderness conquered passion, and by and by I felt his big hand laid gently on my head. "There, there," he clucked, like a mother to her child.

"You're such a good man, McNair," I said, with a catch in my breath. And indeed he is one of Nature's noblemen. We must accept it as her prerogative not to make the rose without the thorns.

"Yes," McNair agreed candidly with my remark; "there

are plenty worse men, even though I have my little faults."

He is very susceptible to praise, is McNair, which is only another way of saying he is a man.

We fell into silence, which I broke after a little by saying: "It's a great weight off my mind. I have been fighting desperately all winter to keep my faith in this cause for your sake, because, at best, it was so hard to have you go. I don't know how to tell you what a happiness the last three years have been to me."

McNair straightened up in his chair abruptly. "Don't," he said, hoarsely; "you shouldn't tempt a man too far."

I sat all a-thrill, hoping in my heart of hearts he would not be able to resist temptation.

The clock ticked along like a railway train in the quiet of the room while I waited with bowed head for whatever might happen.

When McNair spoke again it was in a well-controlled voice of quiet gravity. "Perhaps, when I come back, I may feel that I have a right to tell you what they have meant to a man who had about given up hope. But—well—what I was going to say is that the future immediately ahead will be difficult enough, without adding to our burdens. It is necessary to my peace of mind to have your promise that you will share any worry that may come to you with me."

"But, McNair," I objected.

"Promise me," he said, firmly.

I promised.

*   *   *   *   *

McNair went to camp the next day and I did not see him again before he sailed for England, as the troop train went through in the middle of the night.

He wrote me from Kenora. Such a letter! So full of hope that he would do credit to Canada and the dear ones left behind, and that he might be spared to come back to this glorious country of his adoption and make a place for himself, but if Fate had other plans for him he hoped he would die bravely and so justify my faith in him that way.

Colin, who had taken a room at Mrs. Fleming's since McNair left, came in as I was reading it.

I looked up at him. I was not crying. My heart was bleeding inwardly.

"What's the matter?" he asked.

I opened my mouth to answer, but no sound came. I wet my lips with my tongue. "McNair's gone," I said.

Colin turned a sickly green colour and toppled over. He had been growing very fast lately and was none too strong.

In the effort to revive and comfort the lad I found the only possible ease for my own anguish.

CHAPTER XXIX.
War Profiteers and Soldiers.

It was Sunday afternoon, and Pauline and I were tramping along the dusty road homeward from a long walk, during which, having discussed perfectly innocuous subjects, we had agreed. Unluckily she began to tell me about some investigations that a committee, of which she was a member, had been making into the way the wives of soldiers spent their separation allowances and their time.

"We found Mrs. Thompson was gadding around with other soldiers and Mrs. Davis had bought a new gramophone," she informed me in a low confidential tone; "and of course we explained to them as nicely as we could that they would have to change their ways."

"What business was it of yours?" I inquired, indignantly.

Pauline coloured up. "What do you mean?" she asked, sharply.

"I was just wondering whether you thought the private soldier didn't earn his dollar ten a day by risking his life at his country's behest."

"Of course, but that has nothing to do with it."

"Perhaps not, but I happen to know that one of your committee, who, but the way, is the wife of one of our most successful war profiteers, has two or three young men followers, and another has bought a new limousine in which to go around and advise the wives of soldiers that they ought not to buy gramophones. Has your committee done anything about that?"

Pauline assumed her most bored and supercilious expression. "You make me tired, Aleta," she said; "you don't believe in the war, but you are always professing to be keenly exercised about the wrongs of the private soldier."

"It's not pretending," I said, hotly. "My believing in the necessity of the war has nothing to do with it. The fact is that the country of which I am a citizen has used every means in its power to coerce these men into the army, and then you go prying around into their homes as if they were objects of public charity. You seem to feel that the war profiteer, who makes from two hundred to a thousand percent profit out of the rotten supplies he furnishes the army, has earned his money, and, of course, enjoys the good old British privilege of spending it as he pleases, but the soldier, who is only risking his life, has not a quit claim deed to his dollar ten but his family must also relinquish their personal liberty. What people like you want is a bargain in patriotism in which someone else dies and pays and you gloat."

From that it was an easy step to an argument about the war, which lasted fifteen minutes and ended with our being in such a state of mind that we did not either of us want to know the truth unless the truth justified our point of view.

After we had separated with a curt word of farewell I thought that perhaps if I had been more gentle I might have converted her to my point of view. Possibly she thought the same of me. If she did I fancy we were both wrong, for Nature made her to shout "Hear, hear!" and she made me to shout "No, no!" The bridge between two such extremes is not arguments but generations.

CHAPTER XXX.
Socialism or Christianity.

"What is the solution, Ned?" I asked, as he tramped up and down the room, his hands pushed deep into his trousers pockets, and poured out a flood of invective against the present social system.

"Socialism," he said, decisively.

I shook my head doubtfully.

"Why, I thought you told me the other day that you were almost converted to socialism," he exclaimed, impatiently. Ned sees such ideas as appeal to him with absolute clearness and he has no patience with shilly-shallying.

"That was the week before last," I objected. "Things move so fast these days that I think one out to be allowed to change one's mind at least every two weeks without being accused of inconsistency."

"Well, what's the matter now?" His tone was sharp, for he is rather touchy on the subject of socialism.

"The matter is that you Socialists have exactly the same sense of values as the Capitalist. You are looking for the panacea of human misery in material success. The difference is that you want it for the many while the Capitalist wants it for the few."

Ned whirled around and faced me. "What would you suggest as the alternative?" he asked, coldly.

"Perhaps a return to an old ideal of love as the only

conquering force in the world, and service—not grabbing—as the one source of human happiness."

He leaned his elbow on the mantel-shelf and glared at me. "Good God, Aleta;" he exclaimed, "do you want to return to that Christianity which has put the people in chains to their masters and women in slavery to their husbands?"

"You are speaking of churchianity," I objected.

"It comes to the same thing," Ned insisted. "Found a new church and inside of fifty years it will have become as much the tool of capitalism and the policeman of authority as is the old one."

"Granted," I said, "but found your socialist commonwealth, and in less than fifty years it will have become a much greater tyranny than our present system. This war has thrown some light on the treatment majorities will give minorities when the whole of society can be organised by the government for their suppression. Your socialist commonwealth will be a new kind of hell for anyone who happens to have an original mind."

"Anyway the great mass of the people will have a chance to live decently and get an education."

"But they won't be made either good or happy that way," I remonstrated. "Greed and fear are the emotions out of which have grown the present social structure. Whatever social structure you may erect to-morrow will be dominated by those two emotions unless you substitute for them a new idealism of faith and service."

Ned said, grimly: "Then the situation is hopeless."

"Sometimes, Ned, on rainy days I think it is," I agreed. "I am often overwhelmed by the idea that Nature has moved the western nations to self-destruction because these great materialistic imperialistic world powers stood in the way of a new idealism; that the militant powers of Europe will annihilate each other in this war; and in the next the United States and Japan will complete their self-destruction, and thus leave the stage clear for the middle east, the cradle of all the great religions, except materialism, to lead humanity up to something higher."

"You remember what the old Hebrew poet said: 'Behold the nations are as a drop of a bucket, and are counted as the small dust of the balance.'"

"It is not a pretty thought," I went on, "for if that is the case we Pacifists are wrong in seeking to impede this orgy of destruction. Perhaps in the interests of posterity we would be better employed in cheering it on to its logical conclusion of devastating plagues, revolution and the consequent disintegration of these vast empires into little states."

"You are too much alone, Aleta," Ned said. "You ought to get out and take plenty of exercise. Those ideas are morbid."

"I know," I answered, " the way to be happy is to pick out some formula, pin your faith to it and refuse to think any more. 'The Germans must be wiped out' is simple and satisfying, especially if one happens to be a woman, an elderly man or a cripple. Or if you have another sort of mind, 'Down with the capitalist system.' But when one reads history and sees how often the answered prayer of yesterday becomes to-morrow's curse it gives one pause."

Ned laughed cheerfully. "Then don't read it," he advised. "No use fussing about the centuries ahead. What the world needs right now is Socialism."

"And the next thing after that Christianity and freedom."

Ned frowned.

*   *   *   *   *

The old prophets promised us a new heaven and a new earth. The spiritualists are giving us a new heaven; the British Labour Party has promised us a new earth, but it seems to me that a more pressing need than either is for a new humanity. Otherwise the new heaven will soon become as exclusive and aristocratic as the old and our new earth a fresh monument to tyranny.

But teach every man behind the plough and in the ditch that he is as much the son of God as the Bishop or the Prime Minister, and knows His will as accurately and you will have broken the degrading spell of reverence which binds men's souls in bondage. You have put him upon a plane where no trumpery medals or titles bestowed upon one man by another can exalt him in his own estimation, and where no indignity at the hands of his fellow men can bend him from his principles, or degrade him in his own eyes. Then will men dream great dreams and tell the world of them "and the eyes of them that see shall not be dim, and the ears of them that hear shall hearken."

CHAPTER XXXI.
McNair's Letters.

Sometimes they were only scraps pencilled on the thin checked leaves of a notebook. Occasionally they were written standing up in a hut that was little better than a sieve, as that position, he remarked, philosophically, exposed the least of his considerable surface to the rainfall. Penmanship suffered in these circumstances, but McNair's letters, fragrant with the smoke of his pipe, were like a charm in bringing me happiness.

In one of mine I had asked whether he would care to stay over there for a while in case peace was declared, and he wrote:

"Would I stay long in Europe if peace 'broke out'? I wouldn't stay any longer than to have a bath and a shave, and maybe I wouldn't wait for those if the boat happened to be in a hurry. One doesn't usually dawdle in a graveyard longer than necessary, especially such a crude one as this will always seem to me."

It seemed to me that some of his descriptions of scenes at the front were peculiarly vivid, but I own to being so infatuated with McNair that I am incapable of judging anything of his dispassionately, so I will set one down here.

"For nearly two weeks we have had nothing more exciting than an occasional work party and one march up to the front in the capacity of reserve. We were not required on that occasion, so marched back again.

"It was a fearsome march for a while. The greater part of the horizon looked like the mouth of a furnace. It was one of those still nights, without wind, and the whole country quickly became enveloped in the haze of spring, mixed with the haze of bursting shells, and the flame from the guns and explosives looked more than ordinarily lurid. As our march led us into what seemed the middle of it we may possibly have missed some of the artistic effects, especially when passing through a ruined town one could hear above the tramp of many feet, the clatter of many timbers and hoofs, the crash of shells a few blocks away and the rattle of falling walls, as the very much shattered town was being further shattered.

"However, as I have said, we were not needed, and presently, after midnight, the strafe eased off a bit, and by the time we got back to camp day was almost breaking, and there was only an occasional shot to disturb the quiet of the morning. The country was still clothed in its robe of mist —a fairly close fit—as above it the peculiarly tufted tops of the trees appeared like little green islets in a very still sea."

* * * * *

On one occasion we quarrelled. It was my fault. I sent him an ultra-feminist story in which the heroine asserted her independence of the men of her family in a decidedly forceful manner. She was absolutely right, of course, but my sending the story to McNair was provocative.

He wrote back that he didn't like the story (I knew he wouldn't), that the heroine seemed to him unwomanly and self assertive, and much more in the same vein.

The letter came when I was suffering from a bad cold in the head and was a way behind with my work and exceedingly irritable. It made me very angry. In the furious white heat of my indignation I sat down and wrote him my candid opinion of his outlook upon life.

It is difficult quarrelling by letter, and across the ocean at that. Between this outpouring of my wrath and the reply to it there came half-a-dozen or more every-day letters.

"I've a notion I got a good wigging in your delightful letter," he wrote; "I am not very bright, but I fancy old-fashioned prejudice, keeping an open mind, and similar phrases, heavily underscored, must have had a personal application.

"I hope you won't be more indignant than ever when I tell you that I laughed until I was weak over your epistle and at my glorious escape in not being within reach of you at the moment of writing.

"Go ahead, little woman, and frame a declaration of independence a day, but you won't be independent. Don't you know that people may be more completely bound by their affections than by any legal contract?

"I am sure that if I had consulted my intelligence I would never have chosen you as my friend, but—well— anyway I did, or you chose me, for you began it, of course. At first I had vague plans for making you over. Now the idea of your ever being orthodox moves me to laughter.

"In my old age I am even foolish enough to feel that I shouldn't like the little rebel to be different. When I had made you over you would probably be a person of whom I approved more thoroughly than I do of you, but you wouldn't be you, and nobody who was not you could fill the place in my life that you fill.

"As the chances of losing life increase one sees many things from a different angle. I don't know whether I am making my meaning very clear. I think what I am trying to say is that I can't seem to care as much as I used to about the tools people use, or even the task itself, as about the spirit in which the task is undertaken. I think you must feel this too, otherwise your letters would not be the great stimulus I find them to carry on in a task of which you do not approve.

"Don't be cross at me for laughing, will you? This is a pretty sombre life and it's not often I have a good chuckle."

*   *   *   *   *

One day there came a letter telling me the good news that McNair had conquered his particular weakness for the time being, and, he hoped, for all time. After that there was a warmer and more personal note in his letters which precludes the possibility of exposing them to strangers' eyes. Although no trace had as yet been found of his wife he would soon be legally free, so that we felt the barriers that had divided us disappearing.

CHAPTER XXXII.
Two Telegrams.

I have no patience with the claim that women pay the biggest price in war. It is a lie. My part was easy compared with McNair's, but it was hard enough.

A ring at the door early in the morning. I started up in bed in a cold sweat—was it a telegram? A telephone call late at night and my heart was in my mouth; called out from a meeting I went white.

A strain such as that slowly wears away one's nervous energy, so that the shock, when it does come, finds one with reduced powers of resistance. And it always comes in the end with the suddenness of a bomb explosion.

It was a windy March day, with a cold grey sky. Dirty ridges of snow on the northward looking lawns glowered up at the dark clouds, a defiance of Spring's notice to vacate. The wind, with its subtlety in finding playthings, collected newspapers from the wind alone knows where, and sent them tumbling down the middle of the street or whipped them up and flattened them against a billboard. Then it would go wailing off around the corner, only to come tearing back between two high buildings with a handful of grit to throw in one's teeth. The rawness of it ate into one's very bones.

It was along about three o'clock in the afternoon that I heard a voice outside my door asking for me. There came a rap.

"Come in," I called out carelessly.

It was a telegraph messenger.

I signed the book, took the yellow envelope and waited until the door had closed upon him.

It was from the military office at Ottawa. Lieut. McNair had been gassed and wounded.

I sat down dumb and stricken.

A thousand times I had read gassed and wounded in the casualty lists, and after the first few months of terrible sensitiveness I had grown callous, so that it did not hurt to read those words.

Now they blazed suddenly into life. They meant a human being, kind and loveable, writhing in mortal agony; they meant a man torn and suffering in a strange land, with a wide ocean rolling between him and the ones who loved him best.

It meant McNair fording the waters of affliction alone—unless—unless—Oh God!—unless he had died.

I rose, put on my hat and went into the drear March day to find Colin.

*　　*　　*　　*　　*

Three days passed in a vain effort to learn further details. I cannot tell what I suffered during those days. Hour after hour the rising fever of misery grew, until, proving in excess its own anaesthetic, it brought on numbness; then followed an hour of two of comparative peace while the exhausted nerves gathered fresh energy for protest, and again another long stretch of misery more wearing and exhausting than the last. Impotence is the peculiar sting of this particular form of ordeal, combined with uncertainty, which gives the tortured imagination free rein to create its own hell of horror.

For three days and nights I traversed the battlefields of France. I found McNair in No-Man's-Land, with an arm blown off and gasping for breath; I dug him out from beneath a pile of dead bodies, between trenches, saturated with their blood and his own, which dribbled from the stub of his leg. I stumbled upon his half-naked body in the bottom of a trench, slimy with blood and crawling with vermin, and I raised him up to find half of his face was blown away and that he was stone blind.

I walked alone at twilight over a deserted battlefield, and as I passed a certain place the evening breeze blew to me the smell of carrion, and I turned and looked and there were three black birds pecking at a long dark thing on the ground.

Those were the lesser horrors that I dreamed—the things it is possible to put into words.

*   *   *   *   *

The afternoon of the third day there came another telegram. I was standing out in the general office when they brought it to me. I remember groping my way back to my own room. I remember that I stood with the ugly yellow thing in my hand, choking, until it suddenly came to me that the certainty that McNair was dead would be easier to bear than the awful anguish of the past three days.

I opened it.

It was a cablegram from McNair himself saying that he was in hospital with a thigh wound and out of danger.

That is all I remember.

When I opened my eyes Pauline was sitting beside my bed. She rose, pushed the hair back from my forehead and kissed me. Pauline never kisses me except when I am in trouble, but then she does it with a beautiful tenderness.

I looked about me. It was night and Pauline had turned off all the light in the room except the electric lamp on the table.

"Where's Colin?" I asked.

"I've sent him to bed," she said. "The poor boy is pretty well upset with the double shock."

"I know," I said. "Both telegrams were a shock."

Pauline smiled. "I meant the worry about his two guardians," she explained.

I opened my eyes in surprise. "Did Colin worry about me?" I exclaimed.

"You seem to have completely bewitched those two Scots," she laughed. "Colin came over for me, looking like a grim ghost, and went about with a strained look that was painful to see until I told him on the word of the doctor and the nurse that you were all right. When they were gone he came down and told me he could look after you himself, but I persuaded him to let me stay."

"Dear old Colin," I said.

Almost at that moment the door was pushed open and Colin came softly in, rubbing his eyes.

Observing that I was awake he crossed over to me with long strides, and stood looking down at me self-consciously. He was a big chap now, of a tall man's stature.

"Well, you're a great one to go fainting all over the place," he scolded me.

Talk about the reserved English. They are a gushing river of sentimentality compared with the Scotch. But I love the shy, dour Scot. I never agree with them, for the ones I know are nearly all double-dyed Tories like Pauline and McNair, but I love them.

CHAPTER XXXIII.
The Struggle.

My collapse at the time McNair was wounded was not due altogether to the shock of that event, but because it came on top of an intense emotional struggle which had been going on within me for weeks. As the fury of the war spirit rose it became more and more difficult for me not to protest against utterances which to my ears sounded brutal in the last degree.

One evening, on my way to a meeting at Labour Temple, I turned a corner suddenly and almost collided with one of the city's best known Christian laymen, the head of a large corporation, which at the beginning of the war had reduced the wages of its girls from nine to seven dollars a week and made a front page contribution to the patriotic fund.

"You came around that corner like a German bullet," he said, laughing as he righted himself.

"A sad affair, this war," he continued, "but we've got to go on until we've wiped the last German off the earth."

"Not Christian," he chuckled, in answer to my murmured protest. "I'm not so sure about that. Anyway, I've never had any use for this other cheek business. A little hate isn't a bad thing. We must teach our young men to be brave."

He limped away. He has a club foot.

I continued on my way, sick at heart; also angry. It was so easy, I thought, for a man to be brave with other men's lives. But I caught myself up short at that, for I wanted more than anything else not to grow bitter and cynical. So I forced myself to face the fact that possibly the tendency on the part of cripples to glorify war is due to a gnawing regret at their own lack of physical power. What right had I, who was not handicapped in any way, to judge the mental reactions of a person who had borne a burden like that through life? I tried to reason myself into calmness, which was badly needed in the stormy meeting that followed.

A resolution was on the order paper opposing conscription of men until all the wealth of the country had first been conscripted, and as soon as the secretary read it a little fat woman rolled to her feet and demanded shrilly, "Do you mean to say you would take money we have in the bank?"

The secretary assented.

"Then I'm dead agin it," the fat little woman went on in her high piercing tone. "I've given my son, and I was perfectly willing to do that, but you're not goin' to touch my hundred dollars."

Immediately pandemonium broke loose. People jumped up all over the room and shouted things at each other, without any formalities in regard to the chair. The presiding officer banged the table but they paid no attention to her. It was fifteen minutes before order was restored, and the motion was dropped by tacit consent.

A sullen anger burned on like a live coal, bursting into flame again the moment the meeting was dismissed. People gathered about in little knots and began to talk noisily and excitedly, the object of the talk on both sides not being to arrive at the truth, but to ram their opinions down each other's throats.

"I don't see what you Pacifists make such a fuss about," said a brisk young business woman, who had come into a high salaried position when a young man in the firm for which she worked had enlisted. "Everybody's got to die sooner or later."

I had started to reply when a big, aggressive woman, prominent in our suffrage movement, elbowed her way into the centre of our group and looked about her belligerently. Her eye caught mine.

"Isn't it a disgrace that Congresswoman in the United States voting against war?" she sneered.

"But I thought that in our suffrage campaign you urged that women should be given the vote for that very reason—because they would be opposed to war," I objected.

"I meant that they would be opposed to wars that are past, like the Crimean War or the Boer War, but I never dreamed that women would be opposed to war in their own time or I wouldn't have worked for the vote. The idea!"

There seemed no use in arguing with a woman who could talk such drivel, but when I got home I felt uneasy about it. Was my silence in all these cases a dignified restraint or the same old spirit of cowardice which had dogged me all my life and made me afraid to differ from the accepted thing? I wished there was some way of being sure.

The following week I was attending a farmers' convention in another city, at which a speaker pleaded eloquently for conscription. "Let us have conscription at once, and round up these slackers who are hanging about the city pool rooms," he urged.

Applause that shook the rafters.

A young farmer rose and said, in a slow pleasant voice: "And I move that we farmers keep out of the profits on our grain only the private soldier's pay of a dollar ten a day and give the rest to the government to carry on the war."

Six scattered handclaps greeted the suggestion, two of the loudest clappers being city people. There seemed to me something so sinister in this eagerness to conscript other people's lives and reluctance to part with their own dollars that I went to the reception the Women's Canadian Club was tendering to the delegates that evening with a bitterness of spirit toward the war party in my own country which was no more Christlike than their hatred of the German people.

I found myself, in the course of the evening, in a window recess with one of those commanding society women who always intimidate me. Having discovered that I was a Pacifist she levelled her lorgnette at me fearsomely. "But the atrocities, my dear, the atrocities," she said. "How can you overlook them? Surely people who do things like that ought to be exterminated."

'Well, of course, in the great republic to the south women are said to have thrown babies into the fire at East St. Louis, and leading citizens to have burned a man's eyes out in Tennessee and to have slowly tortured him to death, but they really didn't mean anything by it. It was just their democracy breaking out. In Germany it is their autocracy finding an outlet, and that makes all the difference don't you know."

"Now, why bring up the Belgian cruelties to the Congo natives, and England's flogging and hanging of Egyptians in the Denshawai affair? As I remember it those were only coloured people; also in America. You must see yourself, young lady, that there is a vast difference between crucifying a white man and hanging a coloured one."

"Yes," I said, "I have no doubt their naked bodies have quite a different effect against the sky line."

*   *   *   *   *

If the war party had been completely dominated by this callous, brutal, unimaginative selfishness it would have been a simple matter to oppose them, but mixed with the spirit of profiteering, and blood-thirstiness, and the lust for revenge, and the furious hate there was great devotion and unselfishness and the most frightful suffering.

Pauline was passionately sincere in her conviction that if I had my way and peace was brought about by negotiation the world would go straight to damnation. She was so certain of it that she was willing to resort to means that she knew were wicked to keep me from having my way. And she was stronger than I, because she knew that she was infallible and I did not.

I looked into my own heart day by day and I tried to simplify the issues, but nothing was very clear. I asked myself over and over again whether if I were to go forth and demand that we should have peace I would not be assuming the same omniscience that Pauline assumed in insisting that we must have war? Could one be sure that Nature had not found it necessary to destroy the western half of the world in order to give the power to some more idealistic people? Might not this blind stampede of death have a meaning far beyond the grasp of the present generation? And then again I would ask myself whether these were not merely excuses for my weakness with which I was trying to soothe my conscience for my inactivity, rather than arguments. Try as I would to analyse my emotions I could not be sure. From these fluctuations of my own mind I came to understand many of the inconsistencies on the other side were due to similar uncertainties. I began to see that the little fat woman, who clung so greedily to her hundred dollars, had very likely her great days when she would have given not only her son but her hundred dollars and herself also for her country; and the young girl, who was so well satisfied to take the position vacated by the soldier, probably had glorious hours when she would willingly give it up and go scrubbing for a living if she thought it would benefit the cause in which she believed. I saw our souls swinging on pendulums between the earthly and the spiritual worlds, dominated now by one, now by the other.

So I had blundered along for months, sometimes protesting, sometimes letting things pass and often hating the other side with a ferocity which gave the lie to my pacifist convictions, and always I hated myself for hating. Daily I prayed that if there was a spiritual force that came to the help of human beings it would help me to acquire the spirit of love and mercy and kindness which my mind saw so clearly were the only irresistible forces in the world. So I might have muddled along to the end had not the government begun to forbid us to discuss the war at all, except favourably.

I found my personal telephone was being tapped. One day at noon I remembered that I wanted some information from the military office about Red Cross Nurses for one of our readers, so I used my own telephone. The blur in the sound, which I had noticed for some weeks, came as usual, and the gentleman who answered grew very wrath about the listener.

"There's someone on this line," he bellowed at me.

I answered sweetly: "Yes, there seems to be."

"Get off," he roared; "get off this line." The extra receiver went up with a soft thud.

I could hardly take his message for laughing. But though I laughed there was something in this that bit. I, a Canadian of Canadians, whose parents and grandparents had hewed their way in this new harsh country against great odds; I who had given to its making all of myself that I had to give was being treated as a criminal because I insisted upon discussing the aims for which my countrymen were being asked to die; for which the man I loved lay suffering in England.

A call from the censor warning me that I must say nothing about the proposed conscription measure which would tend to rouse opposition to it if it passed, crystallized my irresolution into action. Since when had Canadians relinquished the right to discuss unmade legislation? Was this Prussia or Canada in which we lived?

Well, anyway, I began to distribute pamphlets demanding that freedom of speech and of the press be preserved, and one day I was arrested and sent to jail.

CHAPTER XXXIV.
Gethsemane.

The second night in jail I walked alone in my Gethsemane, and the Devil of Doubt, almost a visible presence, stood at my right hand and jabbered in my ear the whole long night.

"You've made a hideous mistake," he whispered. "You have mistaken egotism for insight."

"You are the one hundred and fifty billionth part of one thread in the cobweb which time is weaving with the countries of the world as the spokes, centuries as the hitching posts, and the whole human race as the binding cord. And you have decided that you don't like the pattern. That is very droll. You, the one hundred and fifty billionth part of the one thread have decided to change the design."

"But surely," I answered the fiend, "surely when one is willing to give up friends and freedom and social standing, perhaps even health and life itself, that must prove the righteousness of one's cause."

The fiend chuckled. "Leaving out the loss of friends and social standing, are not the other things being given generously and courageously on the other side, and in vastly greater numbers?" he jeered.

I had to admit they were.

"Mark my words," he said, and I could almost hear him lick his lips in the darkness, "all down the centuries the earth has been fertilized with the blood and bones of people who have given their lives freely for ill causes, and Nature has not deviated one hair's-breadth from her purpose to justify their sacrifices. Nor will she for yours. If you're wrong, you're wrong, and if you're right, you're right, and though you died a million deaths you will not alter that."

I sighed, a sigh that came from the very bottom of my heart. "Very well," I said, finally. "I could only follow the gleam as I saw it."

I had peace for a time after that.

*　　*　　*　　*　　*

Just as I was about to fall asleep the Fiend came back again.

"Suppose you are right," he said; "what good do you expect to come from your opposition to authority? Don't you know that the one thoroughly congenial pastime of every succeeding generation is the stoning of the prophets?"

"But posterity always raises monuments to the stoned prophets, so they must accomplish something," I objected.

"True," Doubt assented, "but not to their ideals."

"To what then?" I asked.

"To their stubbornness in clinging to their ideals against coercion. The only thing humanity really admires is obstinacy."

"Before Jesus there was Isaiah, that glorious old firebrand of a Hebrew poet, who put the woes of the poor into song, and after Jesus came Karl Marx, and one day a great orator arose in a temple created as a monument to Jesus, the great apostle of the homeless, and introduced a furious attack upon Karl Marx by that passage from Isaiah:

"'They shall not build and another inhabit; they shall not plant and another eat; for as the days of a tree are the days of my people, and mine elect shall long enjoy the works of their hands!'

"And nobody observed any inconsistency," the Fiend concluded, "because Isaiah and Jesus are a long time dead. A great leader serves only his own generation. Reaction and tyranny fear no prophet but a living one."

"Surely," I questioned, "Jesus is the great exception?"

"He is the great example," Doubt sneered. "Jesus taught meekness and meekness is despised as a vice; he taught the superiority of the spiritual over the material world, and we have a society built on the assumption that might makes right; he taught love and the world is corroded with hate; and our admiration goes out to those who can make others serve them; he taught poverty, and the very church which he founded has grown rich on the fruit of sweat shops and prostitution. Only the other day a Bishop took up a paper and read that poem, which has been going the rounds of the press:

> Said the Pacifist "He only killed my brother,
> and
> Resistance isn't right!
> Said the Pacifist "He only kicked my mother,
> And it's very wrong to fight!
> I think it's wicked rather, to defend
> An aged father, for it might end in a
> quarrel.

> If a Hun assaults your sister (said the gentle
> > Pacifister), turn your other sister to him
> And be moral.

He laughed gleefully. "That's a good joke on Jesus," he said. Then he put on his bishop's garb and went forth to dedicate the church of The Holy Saviour, the last installment of the debt having been paid off by two great financiers as a thank-offering for the defeat of a bill restricting child labour.

"So you see," concluded the Fiend, "there is no immortality for ideas or ideals in martyrdom. God sends his prophets to every generation to translate into the language of their time the few fundamental truths all great men have thought since the beginning of the world, and the story never varies—the world receives them not."

So I wrestled through the night with Doubt, until at last in the dawn I sat up and looked him squarely in the face. "Very well," I said, "suppose I serve only my own generation, I shall serve it with such light as God has given me and, my time being a part of all time, I shall have served humanity."

CHAPTER XXXV.
Out of Jail.

After a week I was let out on bail, to be tried at the midsummer assizes. Some of my radical friends—Ned, of course—came to the jail to meet me, but I would not let them come home with me because I wanted to go alone to Colin. He had come to see me once in jail, but he had been very quiet and I was afraid I had lost his regard. I had not let him know when I would be released, because I thought I would rather talk things out with him alone.

It is not possible for me to do more than set down here the bare fact of Colin's seeming desertion, and that, though I had written to McNair some weeks before I actively engaged in Pacifist propaganda, and quite a long time before my arrest, I had had no word from him. True, I had freed him from our friendship for the duration of the war, as I was unwilling to compromise his position as an office of the army, but I had not expected silence as the answer, and I had thought Colin loved me a little after the fashion in which I loved him. It was difficult enough to bear the reproaches of mother, who had gone to California for her health, accompanied by Jean, and of Jean herself, but for Colin and McNair to fail me—that was my real cross.

It happened that on my way home to my room I met Pauline. She looked the other way, and I slunk past her apologetically, diffidently, and hated myself unspeakably for that inward shrinking.

I walked on, repeating to myself those words of Henley's so dearly loved by all cowards and weaklings:

"'It matters not how straight the gate,
    'How charged with punishment the scroll.
'I am the master of my fate;
    'I am the captain of my soul.'"

I found Colin watering the plants in my room.

"Hello!" I said, with bravado, for I was afraid of Colin.

He looked up gravely. "Hello!" he exclaimed, in surprise. His face looked years older.

I took off my hat, and began to fidget about the room. Colin set down the pitcher and came over and put his arm about my shoulders.

"I want you to talk to me about the war, little woman, and tell me why you feel as you do," he said.

"Come here, laddie," I replied, drawing him over to a chair. We sat down and Colin waited for me to begin, but I didn't begin, I leaned over and patted his hand.

"Colin," I said, "you're McNair's boy. I am not going to use my influence while he is away to turn you against the thing for which he stands, but you have a right to hear the other side. Read any of the radical magazines and books in my little library—"

"They've taken them all away," he interrupted.

"Then read your history and think, sonny. Or read what the editors are saying, and think. Or read the Bible and think. Or read nothing at all, if you like, but just think. Think of your own experience on the playground at school. Think whether it is not true that a soft answer turneth away wrath; whether love or vengeance is harder to resist."

Colin came and knelt beside my chair and put his arms about me and kissed me. "I have been thinking, little mother," he laughed, "until my cocoanut's aching."

I was so happy. It was the first time Colin had called me mother.

*   *   *   *   *

Mrs. Fleming had decided that I was not a desirable boarder, not being "for the Hempire," as she said; so I found a room in the home of a courageous young radical, with a family, who risked his position in taking me in.

That was three weeks ago, and to-day (May day, by the way) my heart is singing as it did that winter night, years ago, when I put my hand in McNair's and felt the thrill of his touch go up my arm and down into my heart.

For I've had a telegram from McNair, asking me to meet him at the station. I cannot meet him. I have promised to address a meeting at the market square at the time the train comes in, but I'll see him in a few hours; I'll feel the touch of his hands and perhaps of his arms and his lips.

Oh, McNair, my heart is as light as thistledown to-day! For all its stupid blundering, what a glorious old world it is!

If only I could meet you at the train. Why not? Why not get someone else to take my place at the meeting? And have them think they have succeeded in intimidating me? Yet it is only once in a lifetime that one's lover comes home from the war.

I'll do it. I can imagine the way you will step off the train, limping a little, and stop and look round, and I can picture the lighting up of your face as you see Colin and me.

If I go to the meeting they will probably arrest me and put me in jail again. And you just home! I'll not go. I cannot go. Surely that isn't necessary. But the whole point of the meeting is that it is to be addressed by one who has been in jail and who refuses to be silenced.

Oh McNair, why did you say that about coming out strong? I don't want to come out strong. I want to be weak and conventional. I want to be happy. Carlyle says: "What act of legislature was there that thou should'st be happy?" None. I do not need Carlyle to tell me that. Laid alongside the great tape measure of eternity the months I might spend in jail would be insignificant. I know that if I were to read the chapter on ghosts, which I am resolved not to do, that fact would emerge triumphant. But I know nothing of eternity. All I am sure of is the little space of time between my birth and death. It may be that the light does not go out at the end, but passes on clearer than ever to the other spheres. It may be that those Orientals are right who believe that we are reabsorbed into some great consciousness. It may only be that we become an undying part of the evolving consciousness of our own world, that as I am the product of all the lives that have preceded mine, so I in turn will go to make a part of all the lives that will come after me. That would be immortality of a sort. But I think it is better than that; a new chance perhaps, in a world where our natural instincts will be less antagonistic to our ideals.

*   *   *   *   *

I have read the chapter on ghosts. Obviously the postponement of our happiness for a few months or years doesn't matter. But when one looks at events in a big enough way to make them shrink to tolerable proportions the good one hopes to accomplish shrinks also. Yet there is still left a tiny residue of God-likeness in sacrifice. So I go to the meeting.

CHAPTER XXXVI.
After an Interlude.

Going through McNair's papers the other day I found this manuscript written by Aleta Dey ten years ago, worn and almost illegible in parts, for McNair had read and reread it. My wife, looking over my shoulder, exclaimed, "What is that, Colin?"

"Read it, dear," I said, putting it into her hands. "I don't think the little woman would mind."

Some hours later she returned, laid it on my desk, and went away again without speaking. She did not refer to it until that evening when we were sitting out on the veranda of our little home overlooking English Bay and watching the clouds play about the peaks of the snow-capped mountains. Then she got up suddenly and came and stood behind my chair and slipped her arms about my neck and stammered: "Would you—would it be wrong—do you think we could publish that story?"

We talked it over for a long time and decided we might, with the conclusion of the sad little tale.

When McNair got off the train the night of that day on which Aleta Dey made the last entry in her autobiography he looked around quickly, and, seeing me alone, he turned pale.

"The little woman?" he asked, anxiously.

I gave him the note she had sent, and he read it, smiling.

"Let us go along to the meeting, laddie," he said, happily.

We went, and as we got down from the street car we saw a howling mob gathered around a small figure on a chair. It was Aleta Dey. As we reached the edge of the crowd someone struck her and she fell over backward. At that McNair gave a terrible cry and began to fight his way to the heart of that struggling, cursing mob, and I followed in the path he opened.

I think the mob was a little stunned to see this huge soldier rush up and gather the tiny form in his arms and kiss the still white face. "Little woman, speak," he moaned. "It's McNair."

She lay like a stone in those strong arms in which she had so longed to rest.

Someone touched him on the elbow. "The doctor's come, sir."

McNair stood by, chewing his military moustache fiercely during the examination. The doctor looked up and shook his head.

"Dead?" McNair asked, hoarsely.

"Not yet," the doctor answered.

McNair laid his hand heavily on my shoulder.

*   *   *   *   *

Aleta Dey lay on a white cot in the private ward of the hospital. Death was creeping slowly up her body from the injured spine to the heart.

McNair sat leaning over the cot on one side, stroking her pretty hair. From time to time he stopped to press his lips to hers, and he kept a firm hold of her little hand as if to draw her back from the unseen world into which she was slipping.

I sat on the other side of the cot, too miserable for words. Aleta Dey was dying. McNair was broken-hearted. Nothing seemed worth while.

"It's nice to have you and Colin at hand," Aleta said, smiling at me.

McNair raised his head and looked at me coldly. "Hasn't Colin been at hand all the time, dear?" he asked, quickly.

"You forget that I have been under lock and key," she answered; "but of course Colin stood by."

McNair said nothing more, but I knew he was not satisfied. Silence fell upon the clean grey little room with the spotless cot and the green shaded light.

A nurse tip-toed in and out again, leaving us three alone once more.

A few intimate friends associated with her in her work had come, said their long farewell and gone away. Ned Grant had been last. When he entered the room McNair stopped and whispered something to Aleta, then he motioned to me to follow him into the hall.

"He loves her, laddie," he said, by way of explanation.

When Grant came out he approached McNair and held out his hand. "Thank you, Captain," he said, gravely. "I don't suppose we could ever be friends, but I understand why Aleta loves you."

McNair blushed like a boy, as he took Grant's hand and pressed it warmly. "I see no reason, sir, why we cannot be friends," he protested. "I shall always have a very warm regard for those who stood by her through this time."

"I'd be glad to—to—have your help later on," he added, as Grant turned away.

Grant nodded, and walked swiftly down the corridor.

So they left us alone with her. With faculties amazingly clear at first her mind turned constantly to the cause for which she had given her life.

"I have been brought into this world," she said once, "without any choice on my part, and have been given a mind, for which I did not stipulate, at variance with my time. Then the world says to me, 'You must stay in this world, for to take your own life is a crime, and you must agree with your time, or if you cannot agree you must make of your life one long hideous lie by pretending that you see eye to eye with your generation."

"I tell you McNair," Aleta's eyes blazed with their former fire and her voice rang with almost its old vigor, "the tenantry of no human body is of sufficient moment for a soul to submit to such an indignity as that. I am not sorry they have foreclosed my mortgage on this house of clay. At last I am unafraid—"

She coughed, turned restlessly and fell silent.

After a time she resumed where she had left off, having apparently been turning it over in her mind: "If there is anything on the other side of death, and I believe there is, it must be freedom. It must be that over here there will not be a thousand souls with clubs standing over one and daring him to tell the truth as he sees it. Otherwise, pray God that the thing that is a few hours ahead of me may be annihilation."

McNair pressed her hand in wordless misery.

About midnight there came a gentle tap at the door and Pauline came in. McNair moved away and she fell on her knees at Aleta's side and kissed her very tenderly. They did not speak of the past. Perhaps it seemed too trivial.

"Write to mother and Jean, Pauline," Aleta said, when Pauline was leaving, "and tell them if they want to do something to please me to be good to my boys."

"I'd like you to write to mother too, dear," she said to McNair, when Pauline had gone out. "She is ill in California partly on account of me, and she and Jean may think of me as having died alone among strangers. I want them to know"—she looked up into McNair's face with an expression of adoration I shall never forget—"that— that I died in the arms of the greatest lover in the world."

And that was true.

* * * * *

Towards morning she spoke again: "Of this I am sure, as I stand at the door of death, or of life, that the only conquering force in the world is love. If I have failed to convince those with whom I have come in contact it is because I have preached love without living it."

"Don't," McNair said, stroking with a shaking hand the beautiful red brown hair; "I can't bear that."

Aleta laid her soft white little hand on his huge one with a gesture of infinite tenderness. "You must try not to mind so much about my going, dear," she urged. "Except for leaving you and Colin I'm—I'm glad to go. I've always been a coward."

Presently she gave a soft little laugh. "I borrow to be born a Tory or brave in the next life."

McNair caught his breath in a dry had sob. "Aleta, my fearless little darling, please don't," he begged. "I can't stand to hear you talk like that."

She smiled at him wistfully and sank into a stupor.

Once again she stirred.

"Don't let any harm come to the boy who—did—it," she whispered. "He risked his life—fair that I should risk mine."

"Very well, dear," McNair answered, master of himself again. It was wonderful the way he kept up through that awful night.

Just as the dawn was creeping in about the drawn shades the light faded from her face, leaving it pale and still.

CHAPTER XXXVII.
McNair Gives Way.

McNair had sat in my room, his head bowed in his hands, ever since I had made him come away from the hospital. Nobody could rouse him. Mr. Grant came to ask about the arrangements. McNair stared at him blankly. The question was repeated.

"Her favourite chapter of the Bible was the fortieth of Isaiah," he said. "Tell the preacher to read that at the service." And he relapsed into gloomy silence.

Grant waited, hoping he would say more.

In the meantime a returned soldier came in and approached McNair, "The boys of our regiment are feeling mean about one of our men having killed a woman. Some of us think it is poor business to go to France to fight for freedom and kill our women off for asking for it at home, no matter how wrong-headed they may be.

"And—and so, sir, they thought they would like to send our band to the funeral to clear the name of the regiment and out of respect to you, sir."

The bowed figure in the shabby khaki uniform did not stir, and I wondered if he had heard.

A stillness fell upon the room. The soldier cleared his throat.

"What shall I say, sir," he began again, shuffling from one foot to the other.

McNair was roused at last. "Don't talk to me of right or wrong," he said, bitterly; "I only know she was the woman I loved—stood by me when I was down. She carried me up to God by her faith in me.

"And—and—now when I've come back to her—" he broke off and his great fists clenched and unclenched spasmodically—"she's gone and I am left alone.

"In the slime and mud of the trenches I used to dream of this coming back. I used to think how I'd care for her and protect her. She was such a wee thing—such a brave wee thing—and now this. She's gone—nothing ahead but a blank."

He fell into a dark brooding silence, as he glowered fiercely, with angry resentful eyes, at the smiling spring day.

The soldier touched him hesitatingly and respectfully on the arm. "About the band?" he suggested diffidently.

"Get out," McNair shouted sharply, roused to sudden fury. "Don't any of you dare to come near her dead body. Don't you dare."

Mr. Grant came forward from the shadow of the window curtain. He was very pale. "I think she would have liked it Captain." He said, quietly.

McNair's head dropped. All the fire and fury left him at once. He turned his haggard, deeply-furrowed face to the soldier. "Very well," he said, in a voice of inexpressible sadness, "let them come."

CHAPTER XXXVIII.
The Funeral.

There is a grandeur in the Dead March in Saul at any time. Accompanied by a tragedy like that of Aleta Dey, which shocks a whole city into thoughtfulness, it is overwhelming.

McNair had elected to walk with me behind her coffin. "There won't be many to do her honour," he said; "let us do what we can. Unless," he added, a little coldly, "you would rather not."

"See here, McNair, what do you mean?" I asked, angrily.

"I think you know," he answered.

"I know you think I went back on Aleta when she was in prison, but I didn't, only I was worrying a lot because as I came near to military age I had to choose between her faith and yours, and I was pretty busy thinking."

"Was that it, my boy?" he asked, eagerly.

"McNair," I said, hotly, "what do you take me for? Didn't she give me the only mothering I ever had in my life?"

He pressed my arm affectionately.

So on the day of the funeral we walked along the middle of the wide clean sunny street, side by side, and after us came many more. McNair was wrong about there being few to follow her. Her death brought hundreds of people with Pacifist leanings, who had said nothing about it, to declare themselves openly. Others, I fancy, joined the procession to clean the hands of the city of the death of a woman who cared more for her principles than for life or liberty. Perhaps because McNair was the chief mourner no attempt was made by Aleta's Pacifist friends to make it the occasion of a demonstration, other than that the ordinary hearse was discarded and the coffin laid upon an open waggon draped in black. It was banked with flowers, people from all parts of the Dominion having paid her the last tribute.

It was very awkward for the authorities that Aleta's lover was a soldier. They were afraid of the funeral, and afraid of stopping it. I think now that they were also afraid of the spirit of tolerance and real freedom McNair preached as he marched with slow heavy step behind that coffin. I seemed to sense a tension in the air as we wound slowly along the street to the solemn throb of the music.

The sound of the drum and bugle died away at the graveside, and the preacher opened the Bible and began to read. The first words that caught my attention were:

> "The voice of him that crieth in the wilderness, Prepare ye the way of the Lord, make straight in the desert a highway for our God."

There was a stirring in the crowd as the words rang out like a challenge on the clear spring air. Some were present who were not prepared to admit that hers was a voice crying in the wilderness.

The preacher read on:

——"The voice said 'Cry.' And he said 'What shall I cry?' All flesh is grass, and the goodliness thereof is as the flower of the field."

Boy though I was, I remember thinking "What's all the fuss about then if we pass like the flowers of the field."

"Who hath measured the waters in the hollow of his hand, and meted out heaven with the span, and comprehended the dust of the earth in a measure, and weighed the mountains in scales, and the hills in a balance."

Imagine the effect of that picture of the immensity of God as we stood beside that yawning grave.

The solemn melodious sentences rolled on, like chords of a mighty pipe-organ:

"Behold the nations are as a drop of a bucket, and are counted as the small dust of the balance: behold he taketh up the isles as a very little thing.

"And Lebanon is not sufficient to burn, nor the beasts thereof sufficient for a burnt offering.

"All nations before him are as nothing; and they are counted to him less than nothing and vanity."

I looked about me, with a new sense of the bigness of things, and I noticed that the tension in the faces of the listeners had relaxed. I am sure they saw, as I did, man's fierce little hates shrinking into insignificance as the Hebrew prophet continued to paint that tremendous picture of the impartiality of God.

> "Have ye not known? have ye not heard? hath it not been told you from the beginning? have ye not understood from the foundations of the earth?
>
> "It is he that sitteth upon the circle of the earth, and the inhabitants thereof are as grasshoppers; that stretcheth out the heavens as a curtain, and spreadeth them out as a tent to dwell in;
>
> "That bringeth the princes to nothing; he maketh the judges of the earth as vanity."

I remembered having read in one of Aleta's articles, "Each little group of grasshoppers has had the impiety to conscript the God of the universe to be the mascot of its armies. He must laugh, if the divine pity were not as far beyond our understanding as the divine habit of thinking in thousands of years is beyond our childish way of imagining that our day is the one day God ever dreamed."

> "Yea, they shall not be planted," rang out the voice of the preacher, "yea they shall not be sown; yea their stock shall not take root in the earth; and he shall blow upon them and they shall wither, and the whirlwind shall take them away as stubble."

I cannot describe the solemn grandeur of that service.

Aleta Dey dead seemed to be more alive than ever. The peace of a new and better understanding settled upon our souls, and sent us away, for the time being at least, cleaner and kinder men and women.

CHAPTER XXXIX.
McNair Passes On.

McNair went home from Aleta Dey's funeral and went to bed. On learning that she might go to prison he had written her at once—a letter which was probably submarined. Then he set about getting his discharge from the hospital in order to come to her. He had not been really fit to travel, and the long journey, with the shock at the end, had proved too much for him. He seemed to lose his grip on life. I tried to coax him to make an effort to get better for my sake, but he would only answer, "You belong to another generation, Colin. You have your own life to make. I'm not afraid but that you'll make a good job of it for the little woman's sake. But she belonged to my time. I can't seem to get started again without her."

Ned Grant came to see him very often and was exceedingly kind. McNair would listen by the hour to stories of Aleta's childhood, which Grant never tired of telling.

Pauline Ransome and Aleta's mother and sister came and did everything they could to soften those last days, but the only bitterness I ever knew McNair to show was in his inability to quite forgive Pauline and Jean for having turned against Aleta, by whose side in a month's time he was laid.

Years afterward my wife and I went out and planted flowers on their graves—pansies on hers and poppies on his, and when we went back two summers later the pansies had crept from her grave on to his and poppies from his grave on to hers. We looked at each other and smiled. "In death they were not divided," my wife quoted, softly.

*   *   *   *   *

Under McNair's pillow when he died was a tattered letter. He used to read it over almost every day, and sometimes, near the end, he would say to me, "Colin laddie, will you read it to me—the little woman's last letter."

This was it:

"Dear McNair,

"I ought to have written this letter weeks ago, but my disinclination was so great I have been trying to cauterize my conscience in this direction. Now necessity leaves me no choice.

"I am obliged to give up your friendship for the duration of the war, because I am about to engage in active propaganda questioning the right of the government to spread among the people of this country the disease of silence, that loathsome cancer of the social body, which breeds fear and suspicion and prepares the soil for violence and scandals and every conceivable form of evil thinking and doing. I am satisfied that the great French philosopher was right when he said: 'A miasma exhales from crouching consciences,' and I would avert this disaster from my country if I could.

"Different as they seem to me it is almost certain that the government will make no distinction between this protest and previous ones I have made against the war, lumping them all together as Pacifism, and the punishment is imprisonment. It might not be well for you to be known to be writing to a Pacifist in jail, so I give you up—until after the war.

"I was deeply touched by your last letter asking that I take you fully into my confidence as to my reasons for opposing the war, and particularly by your suggestion that my reluctance was not very complimentary to your cause.

"I know you think your faith would stand the shock of such arguments as I could bring to bear upon it. I think it might, too, but the consensus of opinion on your side is so overwhelmingly against us that I am afraid to risk it. Since the governments of all the countries concerned in the conflict have decided that with thousands of newspapers and magazines trumpeting the case for war up and down the land the faith of the people in their cause would not survive the publication of the most obscure Pacifist organ, I am not in a position to contradict them, especially as they have much information which the censor has very unkindly denied to me.

"So I'll not give you any of the Pacifist arguments, though, indeed, a cause whose advocates instinctively decide that it can answer its antagonists only with prison has been so deeply censured by its friends that its enemies are left speechless.

"Sooner or later that fact burns itself into the intelligence, and that very tyranny becomes an argument that is well-nigh irresistible. There is no even half-evolved human mind which really respects the bully's logic: 'I'll lick you if you say that again.'

"I think they are mistaken, McNair. I believe if they allowed the most perfect freedom the majority of people would still choose war, for there is something in the human heart which answers 'present' to the roll call of force. All of us, militarist and pacifist alike, have felt the impulse to kill the thing we could not dominate.

"Perfect freedom of speech would make just this difference: no little group of men would be able to keep a country at war for purposes which the majority of the people disapproved. No, it would do more. It would lift the cause of war to a new plane, for we, all of us, in our heart of hearts know that no group of men is sufficiently infallible to be allowed to sift the truth for other men, and we are at bottom deeply ashamed that they should dare to try.

"If I wished for their punishment I should stand aside and egg them on to bring about a revolution by their tyranny, for the people who will allow their consciences to be intimidated are always dangerous people, and the government which depends on their support is playing with gunpowder.

"But I do not believe in revolution; I am convinced that the only permanent conquest is a spiritual one. And, moreover, there is always the possibility that the war party is right and I am wrong, and that if I had my way the march of civilization would be impeded. So I ask only this, that men be given the whole truth. So far the government has never told the people anything until they found it out through the scullery—and then grudgingly. Professing to be engaged in the great crusade to make the world safe for democracy they do not trust their own people with any information which can possibly be concealed from them. Do they imagine Germany does not see the absurdity of this position?

"The people are not swine looking for a pleasant trough in the sun. Let them know all the facts and they will choose the fine and generous thing, whatever that may be. They might choose your way, for I am not as sure of the irresistible nature of my arguments as is the government which would suppress them. But in the full sunlight of truth people would choose the good. This faith in my kind is one clear religion I have left; the only thing which make life tolerable in these hideous days.

"I have told you this because I want you understand how impossible it is for me to remain inactive any longer, though I should like to do so for your sake.

"For I love you, McNair, and I think you know it, but I am putting it into words in case anything should happen to part us for all time. Life has been different for me ever since that night on the train when you turned to me with a twinkle in your eye and asked, 'Did I turn too soon?' I believe I loved you instantly. Not as I love you now after our rich years of happiness, but as my mate, as the one man to whom I could surrender myself as a wife and the mother of children.

"Afterwards I learned to love you as a mother loves her child, generously and protectively as between you and me, selfishly and exclusively as between we two and the rest of the world.

"But at last, McNair, I've grown to love you with the highest form of human affection—I love you as my friend. I love you well enough to give you up for the ends of righteousness, which are greater than this human love of ours.

"It is so great a thing, this love of mine, that I have no shame in speaking of it. I think you love me just as I love you, but if I am wrong in this you will not, I am sure, feel that it binds you in any way, as a commoner man might do. You are too understanding to pity anyone for having loved, even without love's logical fulfillment.

"Just after I had begun to love you I heard some women talking about a woman friend whose engagement had been broken off because the man had learned to care for someone else. And they were sorry for the woman. That seemed to me very strange. What sort of meager little loves must theirs have been that they could pity anyone for having loved as I love you, McNair?

"Perhaps they had never loved and did not know what love does to one's life; that it is a permanent mirage bringing into sight unguessed landscapes in the realm of sympathy and understanding. Nothing of change or disappointment can take away from one this new horizon.

"So I count it the crowning success of my life that I have loved so good a man. It would have been magnificent to have loved any man as I love you, dear one, but to have loved a man who is so much more than just a mate, who has never cheapened my sincerity by flippant word or look, who is the one I would have chosen out of all the world to be my friend—Life has been very generous to give me this. Remembering that, I shall try not to complain whatever lies ahead.

"I shall hear of you through Colin and you of me, and daily—hourly almost—I shall pray for your safety and happiness, my dear, dear one.

"When it comes to a time like this, training in writing helps one very little to reveal one's heart. I don't know how to tell you what I feel other than to say again I love you, and leave you to guess the gestures and caresses with which I would tell it you if you were here. I love you so exactly as a dear old Tory like you wants to be loved that I am almost ashamed of myself; with so complete a surrender of my womanhood to your manhood—

"I must not speak of that. Were I to begin to think how much I want you here—but that way lies weakness. Out of this love of our has come something bigger than human love which I must not betray; something which has inspired both of us to do greater things than either could have achieved alone.

"I am sorry that to-day our causes seem to stand in opposition; but perhaps it is only seeming. It may be that history with its wider perspective will discover them to be two branches of the same tree of freedom, your contending with the winds of tyranny abroad and mine with the winds of tyranny at home.

"And if we should not meet again in earthly life, but should pass on to other spheres of action, we'll do great things together there, dear one, because we've gone through this content with the will for righteousness, and leaving each the other to choose his path."

FINIS.